Kumite

Sean Scott Kerns

DEDICATION

This book is dedicated to my dear friend Bruce who lived life out loud. He read my first four chapters of this book then announced that he loved it and could not wait to see it in print. This is for you Bruce, better late than never.

CONTENTS

Acknowledgments

Foreword   9

Iti   12

Ni   31

San   48

Si   65

Go   77

Roku   91

Siti   109

Hati   130

Ku   146

Ju   164

Epilogue   168

ACKNOWLEDGMENTS

I would like to thank my original proofreader Bruce for his feedback and my favorite proofreader Clarissa for reading this book twice, both cut and uncut. I would also like to thank Lee for designing some of the characters and providing correct terminology. And a special recognition goes to Roz for all her help on this book and the first one.

Foreword

The word *kumite* (pronounced kü-met-tay) is the Japanese word for fight. Not all, but in most martial arts school/studios called *dojo,* (pronounced dō-jō) students are taught how to fight or *kumite* as an application of learned techniques with the principles of fighting: balance, adjustment, independent limbs, rhythm and distance. Often times students learn *kata* (pronounced kä-tä) or *wasa* (pronounced wä-zä), which are pre-designed martial arts fighting forms to get a feel for rhythm and timing while executing kicks and punches. Katas or wasas are choreographed moves designed as a precursor for students to make the transitions from practiced skill to application. *Kumite* is a learning process overseen by the instructor or *sensei*. The *sensei* (pronounced sin-se or sin-sä) explains the rules of *kumite,* as well as coaches the training.

In the *dojo,* the environment for learning is safe and controlled, encouraging students to try new skills and techniques, as well as push themselves. Generally in the *dojo,* students practice fight or spar amongst their classmates at various belt or skill levels. This sparring assist in honing the skills of up and coming martial artists, as well as sharpening the skill of the seasoned martial artists. Seasoned martial artists or upper belts, (black and brown belts), will spar with the novices or lower belts, (green belt and under), so both participating students learn to master control of delivery of techniques and contact.

Kumite is not meant to be brutal, but it **can** be depending on the martial arts style and level of students' control. Along with the *gi* (pronounce gē) or martial arts uniform, protective gear such as padded hands, shins and feet, including the mouth guards and cups, are required in some styles for obvious reasons. Even with protective gear people *can* get injured. Despite the controlled and respectful atmosphere (which is conveyed after opponents *reys* (pronounced rays or rāz) or bows to acknowledge respect), the bottom line is the proficiency to fight is being taught. Fighting is a form of combat and can be used to gain power over an adversary through ferocity. Knowing how to fight can be the difference between life and death in given situations.

Iti

The harsh sounds of a crying man are never comfortable. Detective Miles could understand seeing a man cry during tragedies especially ones that he was the herald for today. A distinguished gentleman in his mid sixties, dressed in a dark pinstripe suit, held his head in his hands. His dyed jet black hair appeared un-kept, which was a contrast to his neatly tanned angular features and manicured hands. Detective Miles recognized him from his television commercials and his appearances in court.

But today, he was just a man whose wife was killed when she lost control of her car in the curve on 16th Street and crashed into the side of an apartment building. A newer model car and a different point of impact might have saved her life. All details aside with none of the gory one to the grieving husband, his job was done. With a business card in his hand, Detective Miles left Bernard Giovonni to his sorrow.

Word got to the karate school about the

tragedy and class was cancelled. Bernard Giovonni's students reacted with mixed emotions. All were grieving for the late Rita Giovonni, a pretty petite blond with dull green eyes. All but one of them wished it were Bernard's demise, his oldest friend, Rocky Plane. Mixed emotions and all, his martial art students got together and rode out to his house to show their support during class time.

The funeral was a quiet, closed casket affair. Pfegan Zimmerman took Rita's death the worst. She was one of the few people from the school that talked to Rita, despite Bernard's efforts to keep her away from the school. They had an unusual common link. Pfegan could not have children and Rita simply did not want any. That is why it came as little or no surprise when Bernard offered to help Pfegan and her husband, Scott with their infertility problem. In an effort to help his wife's friend, he even offered to donate his own sperm, making the two women giggle like schoolgirls.

Scott did not think it was funny. He threw his drink in Bernard's face and swore he regretted the day he had saved the man's life. A decade earlier, Scott had been the pilot on a small cargo plane flying some equipment to an oceanography team when he noticed Bernard adrift in his boat. He radioed back to the local authorities for a rescue. Since that day, they forged a mock friendship. Like his wife, Scott would miss their dear friend Rita. Unlike his wife, Scott had suspicions that Bernard had caused his wife's death, directly or indirectly.

After the services, a small group of students returned to the Giovonni household. As usual, Drew Underhill made a beeline for the library bar. Bernard had known Drew since the day the doctor gave him the slap of life. Drew was the closest thing he had to a son. He hated Drew's drinking as much as he hated Drew's attraction to the mysterious and beautiful Vanessa. Even Bernard's and the late Rita's constant urging, almost nagging, did not discourage the boy from his fondness of the bottle.

There was a light tap at Bernard's shoulder. It was Amanda Dunneski, his dear sweet mistress. He gave her a hug.

"Thank you for attending my love. I know she wasn't your favorite person," he whispered in her ear.

"I came for you. I wanted to be near you. I've missed you." She stroked his genitals between their embrace.

"Oh baby," he moaned, "not here. Meet me in the laundry room in about thirty minutes."

With a final wink and lick of her lips she swaggered away.

"Damn! Your wife's not even cold and she's staking her claim, " Alexis Shaw's comment made Bernard turn to face her, face barely containing his disgust.

"Who let you in bitch?"

"Rita wasn't my best friend, but I think you did her enough wrong when she was alive not to dishonor her in her own home at the repass."

He waved her off, concealing his pain, "Well, she's gone. So how will you blackmail me now? It's a little too late to sell anybody your nasty little information now."

She rolled her eyes, "Please. You are counting your chickens before they hatch. Again. Don't you think the police would be interested in your life? The shady lawyer's wife accidentally loses control of your car, not hers, and is killed. Meanwhile, the grieving husband was just finishing a snack of grapes while doing Amanda Dunneski, college student, part time daycare worker and full time mistress. Why that shit's better than that book by Walter Scott about those colors, Shades of-"

"You'll never tell!" he hissed.

"Oh yes, I might, along with all the other things I know about you and your college dirty deeds. So just in case you're thinking of killing me as well, two deaths in a couple weeks will get you twenty to fifty years, counselor." She gave him her own conspirator wink and foxed away.

Bernard sneaked a peak at his watch and made his way to the laundry room, unaware of Clay Kennedy who stood at the top of the stairs watching their exchange.

Bernard quietly entered the room and closed the door. The smell of her heavy perfume and fabric softener was enough to make him hard. He was glad it was dark. Amanda grabbed his erection and kissed him at the same time. She bit his tongue and the pain only excited him more. When he reached to pull aside her thong, she almost melted in his hands. Now she was rubbing her own juices on his manhood. She had been playing with herself in anticipation of his arrival, just the way he liked it.

Amanda wanted foreplay which meant hugs, kisses and him going down on her. Bernard did not have time for that at this moment. After a few minutes of kissing and caressing, he finally turned her around and shoved her onto the washer. She tried to regain her breath when his erection sprung free. Without a hitch, he lifted her skirt and drove into her from behind.

Her tight wetness was not exciting him enough. He withdrew then drilled into her ass. Her pleas and cries helped him climax in violent passion. He grabbed her hair, to pull her head and cause her back to arch so could Bernard finish with a good thrust deep in her ass. Her partially muted cry was accompanied by his shudders of orgasm. This time, he slowly withdrew and wiped himself on her skirt. "Next time wear real panties. It looked like you didn't have on anything under that skirt earlier. You need to keep up your image. I don't want anybody to think you're a whore but me."

Amanda waited until she heard the door close, to burst into tears. How could a man who often made love to her on rose pedals be so cruel? She did not even hear the door open. When it closed, she whirled around, aware of how she must look. In vain, she tried to fix her appearance, while smoothing her clothes. She faced a slim blond whose face was hidden by the shadows.

"I hope you're all right. That was pretty rough."

Amanda was shocked, "You watched!"

"Well no, I heard you pleading and crying. I came to see if you were in trouble. I heard the scuffling and him slamming you like an animal. He was in and out of here in ten, maybe fifteen minutes. I bet you didn't even get yours." She saw the other woman look at the floor. "Of course not. You know it doesn't have to be that way."

"What are you saying?" Amanda whispered, not knowing what was going to happen next.

"I'm saying it can be gentle and smooth."
The blond turned and locked the door. "By the way, I'm Shannon, from the brown belt section. We've partnered up a few times. I have been watching you for some time. How you prance around Bernard in class. I knew what was going on from the start. You see, you and I are not so different. I used to be you, the flavor of the month. That is until I got tired of being his play thing, used up and never getting my needs met. Someone showed me a different way of getting what I needed. I can do what he can do, only better. Now be a dear and sit on the washer."

Amanda could not resist because she too was beginning to feel like a used play thing and needed a release of her own penned up orgasm. Curious, she did as the other woman said. Shannon kissed away her tears while caressing her breast and buttocks. Shannon kneeled and showed Amanda the difference between a man's and a woman's love making styles.

A week after the funeral, Bernard Giovonni went to work. Barbara Mette's pretty brown face greeted him.

"How have you been Von?"

"Please bring all messages, memos and business into my office," he barked as he kept on walking.

She gathered what he asked for and went behind him. This time she asked a little nastier, "I asked how you have been."

"Okay. Thanks for your support. I know Rita was your friend."

"Clay will be here in ten minutes-"

"God," Bernard sighed.

"-Rocky wants to know if we are still having class tonight. Billy Cannon wants you to call him back. And Craig called. I'll be at my desk." She left barely checking her emotions.

The door to his private suite opened and Craig Black appeared.

"How did you get in here?" Bernard demanded.

"I'm a cop. Remember?"

"What is it? Say what you must and get out."

Craig came over to Bernard's desk. "Look, there's been some talk at the station. A few guys think maybe you had a lot to gain when Rita hit that wall, I mean died."

"That is bullshit. Goodbye Craig."

"All right, but this time it's your ass in a sling. Not mine. I have looked out for you in the past, but this time you are on your own." Before he strolled out the office front door, Craig tossed back, "If you're smart, whatever or whoever you are doing should stay quiet until the speculation blows over. That's all I'm saying, *sensei*."

Next, Bernard called Billy Cannon. Good old Billy was back in business now that he recovered from his cold and was back at work. They were to meet at the sports pub by the highway patrol station at one o'clock. Another call was placed, this one to Rocky. Class was on. Before he could call the insurance company, they called him. Formalities. In less than a month, he would receive three million dollars. No small change for wife number two. After his notification of such good fortune, the rest of the day would be a breeze despite the unanticipated meeting with his simple nephew.

That night they stood before their instructor, almost motionless. The top ranking black belt was Alexis Shaw. She looked like the typical Oriental beauty with raven hair framing an oblong face. She was thin and agile, quick and deadly as a snake. Beside her was Craig Black, the dirty cop. Over six feet, barrel chested and chestnut hair with rugged ex-football player scars. He looked more like a quarterback than a cop. Next in line was his secretary, Barbara Mette, a curvy beauty with coffee colored skin and salt and pepper hair that brushed her shoulders. She was an amazing beauty with hazel eyes which gave her a stately air. She was as professional in class as she was in his office.

The man that stood beside the two made Bernard's stomach turn on occasion, TJ Willis. He was a gangly, awkward coppertop with acne scars and an annoying personality to match. He looked like a nerd who discovered the gym.

Some nights when they worked out, Bernard thought about accidentally on purpose hurting TJ. But then gone would be his entertainment connection and lens man.

Beside him were the Zimmermans, Bernard's personal pilot Scott and his precious wife Pfegan. Standing beside each other, they looked a hotdog and hamburger on a plate. Him, rail thin, lanky, red headed and pockmarked from years of smoking. Her blond, short, square shaped like a box of cereal with a pretty face. If only she would leave that stupid Scott, she would have the baby she longed for so much.

Finishing out the front row was his godson, alcoholic Drew Underhill, who favored his deceased mother and his weird ass nephew, Clay Kennedy, who favored that creep husband of Bernard's sister. Drew looked like a young, darker Ali while Clay wished he looked like Ali. Clay was pale and out of shape to be in a martial arts class, let alone a black belt. Weird just like Bernard thought, shaking his head.

The only black belt in the second row was his future conquest, Dr. Nicole Thorpe. She was tall for a woman, above average height with dark ash brown hair that was currently up in a ponytail. She had a true old school bottle shape. He loved to watch the way her breast moved when she kicked.

Shannon Enlow, yesterday's whore, started the brown belts. She was a skinny dirty blond with breasts too big for her frame. Bernard should know, he paid for them to get the size he liked. That was all she had going for her now because other than those perfect size 34D, she looked used for a woman in her late twenties.

The good Billy Cannon was next to his former mistress. He reminded Bernard of a circus bear with ginger hair, cumbersome and sometimes uncoordinated. Then, there was his least favorite person Vanessa Hollingsworth. He hated her, although he could not deny her striking appearance. Her Hispanic and Asian heritage gave her a most exotic look. If she was not helping Alexis blackmail him, he might have considered her a candidate for his pleasure. But she was part of that college gossip that pique her partner in crime's interest about his activities. Damn her and the scandal she held over his head.

Last was his current mistress Amanda Dunneski. Brunette, small, curvy and docile; just the way he liked his women. Well, he liked obedience by force, but docile would do for now. Bernard *reyed* them in and the advanced class began.

Tonight's workout was light. The class paired up which gave Bernard an opportunity to be paired with Dr. Nicole. She was so poised and professional. He could already imagine her squeals of pleasure coming from her tight mouth. Tonight she wore a tank top under her uniform. Her breasts threatened to spill out. His mind drifted to wanting to taste one. As if reading his thoughts she said, "I've already laced my breast with strychnine, so touch them and die."

"You don't know what you're missing," he sighed.

"Yes, you do. Not much" Vanessa shot from beside them.

Jesus, he hated that woman.

The class broke up quickly after dismissal. Bernard and Rocky went for drinks just like old times. The two old friends appeared polar opposites, Bernard tanned, distinguished obviously of Italian decent. Rocky completely gray, including beard, with a stocky build. He grayed early and was completely gray by his thirties. He had worry lines around his brown eyes which added to his already weathered look. Sitting at the bar of a local hotel, Robert "Rocky" Plaine leveled with his friend.

"Bernard, looks like Rita's death would be a reason to take a break old man."

"Whatever. Look, you know just as much as I do that Rita was beginning to get unhappy. It was getting harder and harder to keep my taste in check. I told her to find a lover, even encouraged her to find a younger man. I didn't care as long as she was happy and out of my own personal affairs. Dammit, I just didn't have time for her like when we dated."

Rocky sighed, "Yeah, but she was a sweet person."

"Here's to her." Bernard raised his glass. Rita was indeed a sweet person. When he first saw her, the attraction was immediate. Rita had a lovely personality and dynamic looks with honey blond hair, sharp green eyes, dangerous curves on her five and a half foot frame. Her calm and quiet demeanor made him want to change to be a better man for her. Her love was almost enough to sustain him for years. She was his queen, placed high on a pedestal for the entire world to marvel. More than that, she was one of his only true friends, turning her heads at times so he could be himself.

"Have you given much thought to totally giving up the school?"

Bernard eyed his friend closely. "Do you want me out of the picture that bad?"

"No, if I wanted you out, you'd be dead." Rocky chuckled at his own joke, though Bernard did not. "We had discussed this many times before Rita died. I was wondering had you given it much more thought."

"Rocky my friend, I'm a single man now. That karate school is a gold mine of sweet young ass. Why haven't you tried any one of those bitches for yourself?"

"Well, Bernard, you slept with almost everyone there. I don't take kindly to sloppy seconds."

"Hell man, once they've had me, they're all broken in for the next one. Just right for you to do some picking and start to sticking." Only Bernard laughed at his lewd comment. Rocky could only shake his head.

Rocky met Bernard while training in Florida. Bernard was in college and training on base with some army buddies on the boxing team. The two trained together for a few months and eventually became friends. Shortly after Bernard's fight, Rocky was stationed in Korea for a year. During this time, Rocky took Korean martial arts while Bernard graduated and moved to Japan to continue his study of the martial arts.

Some years later, Rocky's military career was cut short by a helicopter accident that left him with seizures. After almost eighteen months of rehab, Rocky's seizures were under control. He and Bernard corresponded the whole time. Bernard was now back in the States going to law school and considering moving to Scarborough to open a karate school while practicing law. He wanted his friend to move and start the school with him.

So Rocky moved to Scarborough to teach karate classes at night while attending classes at the local university during the day to earn a degree in urban planning. His seizures came and went, delaying his plans to immediately start a second degree.

By the time Rocky had started graduate school, Bernard had promoted his first class of black belts. The karate school began to include boxing and expanded its activities to the local university. There were six classes, one for children, one after school, an adult beginner, an adult advanced, a kickboxing class and a satellite class on the college campus. Rocky stayed true to his roots and taught the kickboxing, after school and beginning adult classes. Bernard taught the adult advanced class and Craig, the children's and campus classes.

When the campus students began to come to the school, Rocky began to see a change in Bernard. Ever the skillful teacher though, Bernard eventually became mentor and absent father to the young and hungry for the knowledge and discipline of martial arts.

However, he also developed a second darker persona, secretive and manipulative.

As the decades went by, he seemed to become very discriminative against the males and overly flirtatious with the females. Rocky was not sure if this was the cause of Sherry, Bernard's first wife, leaving him or just the demands of his job. Rocky also saw that when they went out, Bernard took home some of the college students from class. He knew Bernard was having sexual relations with some of the female students. Sometimes they came back, however, most did not.

The school had good years and bad years. A loyal few became family. When Rocky tried to get Bernard to change, he blew the suggestions off. On a good night, Bernard was his old friend again, being himself and instructing a great class. Those times after class they would go out for drinks where he would express remorse and talk about his love for Sherry. On a bad night, Rocky did not care to know what he was doing beyond the dojo and could really imagine life without Bernard's particular self satisfying escapades.

Ni

"Mister Dan Brane to see you," announced Barbara from Bernard's phone on his desk.

"Thanks."

Barbara ushered in the human form of the Greek god Adonis. Dan Brane was a tall, blue-eyed confident man with a platinum blonde mane. He was dressed comfortably in khakis and a dark blazer. He gave Bernard a firm handshake and flashed a winning white smile.

"Mr. Giovonni."

A much-impressed Bernard replied, "Mr. Brane, please have a seat. Tell me more about your proposition."

For the next thirty minutes, the two men engaged in conversation. Dan was a student at the local university. His system was Mykuan Ryu. For a few months now, he and eight other students had been working out in the extra lobby of one of the coed dorms. After talking with Vanessa Hollingsworth, Dan thought his style was adaptable to Bernard's.

Bernard asked Dan if he had heard about the university's karate organization. He explained he had formed the organization some years ago and it once had a formidable competition team. For some time now, no one had been interested in restarting the team. Between the two men, they worked out the details for Dan to be the university trainer and liaison for the school. The deal was signed with a drink and a handshake.

The following week's class was buzzing when the new people came in. Barbara had already told the women about Dan. Bernard started class then introduced the new students. Class went a little slow as it was more of an introduction than a workout. Each university student was paired with one of Bernard's students. The experience turned out well. At the end of class, mostly everyone stayed after to talk, except for Dr. Nicole. She had business to attend to at home.

Nicole arrived to an empty home, took a shower and changed. Billy soon showed up with take out from their favorite Chinese takeout place. They ate and watched science fiction reruns. While he went to take a shower, she cleaned up then went to the bedroom to wait. Dr. Nicole was feeling playful. She waited until she heard the shower turn off, and then crouched behind the dresser wearing only a teddy. Billy came out looking for Nicole. Puzzled, he sat down on the bed to dry off. Nicole quietly eased from behind the dresser towards the bed, slipped in behind him, and began kissing his neck.

Playfully, he grabbed her and pushed her to the bed. "Do you know what I do to playful kittens?" he asked. "I eat them up."

He kissed her throat as his wet hands worked up her thighs.

"Hey mister, you're getting the sheets wet." She picked up his towel and began to dry him off. Next, she massaged his body until he was relaxed yet horny. They made slow sensual love that exhausted her. As they laid in each other arms, Billy turned to Nicole. "You know, I am tired of dealing with Bernard. He gets more demanding each time he needs a supply or information. This sounds awful, but I wish it was him who died and not Rita."

At that, Nicole sat straight up and looked into his brown eyes with her cold blue ones. "Be careful what you say and who else you might say that to. Why would you say something like that anyway?"

Billy shrugged and closed the subject for the night by saying, "Just tired."

The next day at work, Dr. Nicole received a beautiful bouquet of roses. The card read 'You are beautiful as the day I first laid eyes on you. Meet me at Raul's for lunch'. It was unsigned.

Dr. Nicole smiled. She was wearing that same smile a little after twelve seated at Raul's Italian Eatery. Looking at her watch, she picked up the menu.

"I'm glad you could make it." Bernard took the seat opposite her.

Behind the menu she was shocked. Her shock turned to seething anger. With a quick decision she dropped the menu and said, "Just what do you want from me? Really?"

"Well hello Bernard. It's good to see. Hello

to you too Nicole. You look lovely as usual," he mocked. Feigning innocence, Bernard spread his hands, "Really, I just want to get to know you."

"Your extent of knowing me is in class. Enjoy lunch." She collected her handbag to leave, but he held her hand in place.

"Actually, I called you here for other reasons." Ignoring her smirk he continued, "One of the new university students wants extra help in our system. I personally don't have time to assist in her training. Since you're one of the senior black belts and your extra time is not used to please me, what do you say?"

Nicole rolled her eyes at his arrogance. "What kind of time? My weekends are my own. Also, are we talking about, the usual two nights or four?"

"Whatever you can spare, just once a week or so, if that's all you have. She needs that extra time to distinguish their kicks from our kicks, their *katas* from our *katas*. I'll set it up for you two to talk tomorrow night."

"All right Bernard," she sighed then

snapped before leaving, "This better not be another bullshit setup like today."

The next night, she was introduced to her new student, Pamell. After class, Nicole evaluated the girl's level and made plans to meet her next week. The weeks to follow were set up in a pattern. Every Tuesday and Wednesday, Nicole and Pamell worked out. The girl seemed to be coming along just fine. Plus, Nicole was really starting to like the girl. She was hard working, honest, and seemingly very wholesome.

The more they spent time together, the more she learned about the college junior. Pamell was from an immigrant family. She came to America around the second grade but could not advance in school until she mastered the English language. She graduated from high school in a busy coastal resort city and got a full scholarship to college for her grades. Some weekends she would go back to the beach to help her parents with banquets at their family hotel business.

With the money she earned, she bought a car that always seemed to break down. Sometimes, she would call Nicole for a ride to class. More than happy to help her, Nicole offered any help she could give beyond karate class.

About three weeks into their training, Nicole began to notice a change in the college junior. When they were doing wall stretches, Nicole put Pamell's leg up on her shoulder, and the girl winced in pain. Thinking maybe Pamell had a leg cramp, Nicole moved on to another, lower leg stretch. Still, the young woman seemed a little distracted. Less than an hour and many frustrating tries later, Nicole sent her to the weight room for twenty minutes on the leg machine.

Nicole pondered this change in Pamell while doing her own *kata*. The phone rang, jarring her concentration. She ran to the office to answer it. "Hello, karate school."

"Nicole," she was surprised to hear Bernard on the other end, "how's everything going? Is Pamell working out okay?"

"Yeah, sure."

"Is she staying for class tonight?"

Annoyed, she snapped, "I would assume so.

You did make the mandatory attendance promotion policy. Plus, I gave her a ride. If I stay, she stays. Why? Aren't you going to be here?"

"Of course!" he sounded almost giddy. "Why wouldn't I be?"

"Whatever," Nicole rolled her eyes. Jerk. "If you don't want anything else, goodbye."

During class that night, she noticed Pamell with that same distracted demeanor, only it totally ruined her work out. Nicole dismissed it as having a bad night.

She did not think anything else about the incident until the following week after practice. Pamell was changing in the dressing room when she walked in. The girl quickly covered herself up, but not before Nicole saw the fading bruises on her back. Her professional instinct alarm went off, but she played it cool. Since they rode to practice together, Nicole would wait until the right time. On the way home she innocently asked if she could use the girl's phone to check with her answering service, knowing her cell phone was in her purse. When she got a positive response, she knew what to do.

Once she had used the phone, she powered it off then turned to Pamell. "I have only known you a very short time, so I hope I am not intruding. I am coming to you as a friend and a doctor. Where did you get those bruises? From what I saw, they looked like teeth marks and scratches. That added to the fact that you have been awful spacey all of a sudden. You act like someone who has been through a trauma, like rape. What happened?"

Pamell looked away. "It's nothing. Playing with a neighbor's dog."

Nicole went on to force the issue. "By law, I am required to report such an incident or any other incidents. Now, you can tell me as a friend and confidant or I can go to the police."

Pamell's head whipped around, tears brimming in her eyes. "Please don't! I cannot disgrace my family. I cannot bear anymore shame."

"There is no shame in telling me. I am not here to judge you. I just want to find out what happened and how to help you deal with it."

"I will only tell if you promise not to tell a

soul, especially not at the *dojo* or university. My exams are in a few weeks and I have worked so hard for my GPA this semester," she sobbed.

"Fine," Nicole coaxed, "it stays right here."

Pamell began her story with Bernard taking her home last Tuesday night after class because she agreed to help him with some typing. He had told her that students would sometimes earn money by typing up briefs when the girls in his office got overwhelmed by the work load. Before last Tuesday night, she had been at his house a few times typing some work. Once or twice he came on to her, but both times he had been drinking. One time, he was massaging her neck and began biting her earlobes and facial area. When it got rough, she told him to stop. When he got hold of her again, he began trying to take her clothes off. When she protested, he attempted to pull her pants down. When she screamed, he seemed to come back to his senses and apologized. On the ride back to her dorm, he apologized several times; therefore, she dismissed it as him being drunk. Plus, he paid her triple the charge for typing.

Last Tuesday night, he said he had some

work for her at his house. It was due the next morning so it was a rush job. Once she got to work, he disappeared. He came in once to put down a box and check her progress. She was proofreading her work when he returned. He had showered and had been drinking. He approached her asking how her sessions with Nicole were going. She answered him without looking up.

Before she could react, he turned her chair around and pulled her roughly to him. He told her there was one sure way to pass her belt test and that was to sleep with him. He said if she did not, he would make sure she would never get her belt and use his friends at the university to make sure she would lose her scholarship. Then, he would send the health inspector to her family's business to find a problem. She could avoid all that, if she would just do it this one time. Her answer was her compliance, when he forced her down on her knees. He pulled down his shorts and stuffed himself into her mouth. He forced himself in and out, ignoring her gurgling and gagging. At the point she thought she could take no more, she sank her teeth into him, as a defensive reflex. That earned her a hard disorientating slap.

He withdrew and moved away. But before she could catch her breath, he was pulling her up by her hair to kiss him. His kiss became gentle, even playful. He seductively pulled off her T-shirt and bra, humming as he did so. He caressed her breast, filling his mouth with each one while rubbing her back. He pushed her arms over her head as he pushed backwards against his desk, molding his body to hers. When she thought that possibly this could be bearable, he clamped a pair of leather handcuffs around her wrist. When her eyes flew open in surprise, he kissed her face gingerly. She tried to protest but he covered her mouth. Then he forced a red rubber ball in her mouth. She tried to move her arms and they did move. Only further apart. She was handcuffed to some kind of expandable bar. Now realizing she could not move her hands or scream, she knew she was in trouble.

Bernard stepped back and laughed. He then pulled her to the floor, using the bar, as he dragged her to the couch. Lifting up one end of the couch, he secured the bar under one leg. She could not see what he was doing, but he returned with some sex toys and a video camera. He sat the camera on a tripod and began undressing. Before turning on the camera, he put on a black leather mask and pulled out mini clamps for her nipples. His tugging on the connecting chain brought tears to her eyes.

She lost track of time over the next course of events. He continually and sadistically violated her, only stopping to spank her or bite her. At one point his scratches drew blood. Pamell said she handled this by just zoning out. Sometimes, she thought she had passed out, only to be awakened by a mini spanking. During this time, he bragged about how she was the best he ever had and how much he wanted to do it again Thursday night. Finally, he said he would take out the ball if she agreed not to scream. If she did, he would pinch a nerve that could paralyze her arm. He pinched a nerve under her arm to prove his point. He removed the ball so she could breathe.

After what seemed like an eternity of him pounding away, he pulled out then stuck himself into her mouth and came. She began choking it back, but he commanded her to swallow. Bernard pinched a nerve in her arm and she did as she was told. Spent, he got up and went into a side room and brought back a chair. Gently as if she would break, he released the bar from the couch leg. He collapsed the bar and sat her in the chair. She heard the sound of running water. He came back with a washcloth and began to clean her. First her face, then her body, moving carefully over the bruises, he washed between her legs and down to her feet.

With that done, Bernard got her some juice from the mini refrigerator. He held it while she sipped from a straw. During this time he talked kindly to her, explaining how the first time he always got his and next time he would make sure she was happy. He caressed her face and said he had something for her to do while he took a shower. This time he shackled her leg to the chair and turned her around to face the TV.

He put in a tape of him with some short Asian. She was handcuffed in the fetal position. He took her repeatedly, anyway he liked. When he was done, he gave the raven haired beauty the same bathing treatment he gave to Pamell in the exact same chair Bernard just put her in. He bathed her then let her watch a video of a young black girl.

He came back in the frame from somewhere and began talking gently to her. He caressed her and buried his face between her thighs. That turned into biting again. The girl on the tape seemed to enjoy it. She climaxed again and again, body convulsing. Her enjoyment turned to surprise when he gagged and blindfolded her. He opened the door and four older men came in. Pamell recognized one of them from the university's football team coaching staff.

They took her two at a time with Bernard watching. The little Asian girl screamed against the gag to no avail. Bernard bent over and whispered something in her ear then took the gag out to kneel over her and put himself in her mouth.

Pamell had never been so disgusted at the sight of these men pawing and destroying this small woman. She closed her eyes to shut out the sight, but the woman's struggle could still be heard. She opened her eyes to a new sensation, arousal mixed with fear. Bernard was kneeling in front of her, kissing her thighs. "Please, please, don't do me like her."

He laughed, "Oh no dear. There's no one

here but us."

He continued to taste her with his magic tongue, driven by her ragged breath sounds. His tongue felt like pure liquid. She could not help but to climax over and over again. Then, without warning the biting began. She should have known from the video. He took one opportunity to bite her hard enough to bring tears in her eyes. She opened her eyes and the video was still playing. This time Bernard was pounding into the girl as the men each held an arm or leg. Pamell began to cry. This seemed to anger him. In a flash, he undid the ankle shackles and yanked her out of the chair. He pushed her onto the top of his desk, with only a wet finger raked across her ass, he sodomized her bent over on his desk.

Pamell could not remember much after that. He dropped her off at her dorm, clothes intact. Before he left, he told her everything was on tape and threatened her and her family again. Somehow, she made it upstairs to her room and the shower. There, she vomited repeatedly, contemplating suicide. She returned to her room and skipped class the next day. Between crying and sleeping, she pulled herself together enough to come to practice with Nicole. She was determined to move on with her life.

When she finished her story, she was in tears and Nicole was mortified. In her career as a doctor, she had never heard such a story. She too began to cry. Crying for Pamell, crying for countless other women Bernard did this to and crying from sheer anger. She could kill him at that very minute, but first she had to deal with the situation at hand.

First, she made Pamell promise to go to the infirmary the next day. She needed to get a thorough examination. Nicole promised she would call after that. Next, she and Pamell decided Pamell should go to counseling. Then, she decided to help Pamell get her car fixed. Finally, she made the promise of a lifetime; that Bernard would never do those things to another human.

San

"Honey," Nicole asked one night, "is Bernard the only reason that we're not married?"

Looking up from his book, Billy frowned. "No, but he's about ninety percent of it."

"You haven't told me how you got mixed up with him beyond class."

Sighing, Billy marked his page and turned to face Nicole. "About five years ago, I became disgusted with the medical school's research projects and began saving to quit my job. I stopped coming to class because I couldn't afford monthly cost of the *dojo* plus the expensive divorce my wife was dragging out. Bernard came by the house one night inquiring why one of his most promising brown belts stopped coming. I told him about my work and impending financial situation. He told me he knew some people at the new pharmaceutical company and could get me in if I would repay the favor."

"Somehow, he got me in for an interview and the job. In return I told him about the products the pharmaceutical company was producing which affected the stock market. I would tell him when there was increase or decrease in the product orders; thus affecting not only our stock but competitors as well. When I thought I had given him enough information to return my favor, Bernard revealed that I had been giving him what is known as insider information, which is against the law. He, being a lawyer, would report this to the DA's office and the Feds. However, it would be our little secret plus Bernard would still get goodies of any new sample drugs especially any male enhancement product and sedatives."

"So here I am now-two steps from jail, rebuilding my account slash finances from when my ex-wife cleaned me out, and never being able to be with the one true love of my life."

Billy's tale hurt and angered Nicole, almost as much as Pamell's story. She decided to approach the subject of revenge lightly with

Billy. "What if I could teach Bernard a lesson?"

Billy raised an eyebrow, "What kind of lesson?"

"The kind an overbearing, arrogant man like him needs."

"You would really . . . um . . . really . . . cross . . . him?" Billy licked his lips nervously. "I mean, you're serious about this?"

"Yes."

"But why? I've been dealing with this for years. Don't do it because of me."

She smiled, "You're just another reason. I was a black belt when you came, remember. I've been in this system a long time. I have seen and heard things that people don't think I know. When I started, Rocky taught class and Bernard taught when he felt like it. When women started taking interest in what the school had to offer like women's boxing and self defense classes, Bernard started taking a special interest in those classes."

"After his last divorce, he was barely under control. When he married Rita, he got better, then he got worse. Just in the past couple of years, he has been blatant and unbearably aggressive. Do you know how many times I have had to warn him off? When you took an interest in me, he became obsessed. I knew Rita somewhat. Can you imagine how Bernard's constant flirting with women hurt her, even with him trying to hide it! I feel it's time to show him that enough is enough. And if I have to cross him to stand up to him, then that's what I'll do."

"Honey please, I do not want to lose you over this . . . whatever you are going to do."

Nicole kissed him, "You won't. Just help me and I promise you the happiness we both want."

The look on Bernard's face when Nicole said she would go to dinner with him was priceless. During dinner she was pleasant. They discussed the girl she was working with, class, current events, mutual acquaintances and work. Nicole held her composure and waited for the right moment to suggest they continue the evening at her place. The look on his face when she invited him back to her house matched the one he had when she accepted his dinner invitation. Once there, Nicole made sure he was seated on the couch and went to get wine. After a few glasses of wine, Bernard was drunk and compliant.

Sometime later, Nicole startled him awake. "Bernard! Look what time it is."

He sat up unsteady, when he realized his shirt was off, he became a little more alert. Bernard looked from Nicole to the empty wine glasses on the table. Then he looked back at her and the fog of confusion was gone. Her shirt was gone too and her bra torn. Not quite this time, he thought as she turned away.

"It's late and things seemed to have gotten out of control. I think you better go." She rose, grabbing her shirt from the floor.

"Yes," he agreed, retrieving then putting on his own shirt. He went to kiss her but settled for a peck on the cheek. He smiled then let himself out.

Less than fifteen minutes later Billy

returned. "Everything go all right?"

"Yes and thank you. I could not have done this without you."

"Oh angel," he hugged her, "it's not over just yet."

Nicole smiled, "Yes, but if this works out like we planned, we can be finally together with no threats from Bernard."

With one final kiss, they went to bed.

The next night in class, Bernard was different. He was, well, normal. He taught class like a legitimate instructor, not like some alley cat in heat. There were no lewd comments or jokes toward Nicole or anyone else. Nicole was puzzled until she went to her car. There was a note in the door of her silver 370z.

"Looking forward to seeing you again. How about Saturday? Call the office tomorrow. B."

Nicole snorted. Bernard was his usual presumptive self, but why the act in class?

"You don't know what he was like in class," Nicole explained to Billy once she got home.

"Then this note."

Billy sighed, "He's just playing coy. Come on baby, look at him or at his track record. He's planning something for you."

"Or, he doesn't know how to take it. Think man. He's pursued me for years and suddenly I give him the time of day. He doesn't know what is going on. I mean look at this note. This is the action of a teenager." She took a swallow of wine. "He may not believe I'm interested in him because he knows we are together."

Billy smiled, "Well, let's give him a reason to believe different. First, go out with him, but not on Saturday. Pick a day between classes, that way he'll have plenty of questions for you to validate your interest."

Monday night, Bernard met Nicole at The Suite. He was so charming, as charming as the devil himself. When he brought up Billy's name, Nicole made a face. Bernard pounced at the moment, "Why the face? Is everything all right in Happily-Ever-After land?"

"It's none of your business. Just drop it."

"Are you sure? You can talk-"

"I said drop it!" she snapped.

Smirking, Bernard spent the rest of the night being polite and massaging her thigh.

The Nicole and Billy performance began Tuesday night. Gone was their socializing before class as a couple. Gone was their attempt to stretch each other. He stretched with Scott and left her with Pfegan. Their friends had no clue, so their genuine reaction helped convince Bernard. He did a good job of trying not to show interest. When the class was over, Nicole said her goodnights and went to the car. Billy came out of the dressing room looking for her. Rocky said she left. To this Billy swore as he left, leaving Rocky puzzled along with the people around him as well.

Thursday night, the second act of the Nicole and Billy performance opened, beginning with the same distant behavior. This time, after class was over, she went in the office to make a call. Billy came in and they had a small argument. They left together after strained goodbyes. Knowing the stage was set, Nicole called Bernard and they went out Friday night. She pretended to be moody and tired. Bernard commented on both, "You don't seem yourself tonight. You seem tired."

"I am. Life is stress."

"Job stressing you out?"

"Not really. College kids are as they have been for five years."

A little more quietly he asked, "How are things at home?"

"They could be better. They could be worse. Hell, I don't know and I don't care." She took a gulp of wine for dramatic effect.

Bernard leaned forward, interested, "I know he's not abusing you?"

"As if! But with that bitch calling the house, what's the difference?"

Bernard frowned, "Billy is cheating on you? That doesn't sound like him."

"Yeah, well that's what I thought too. I could be wrong. I just don't know what to think. Look, let's not talk about this anymore. It'll spoil our dinner."

He let it go, but by now Nicole knew she had him hooked. All she had to do was feed him a little more story each time. She fed him a little more over wine. Tonight was not a necking night. Nonetheless, she still had time to do what was needed. After a lengthy kiss, he said goodnight and they made plans for Saturday.

Saturday night, she made them dinner. After dinner, they talked for hours. Eventually, the talking led to something else. In the middle of undressing a nervous Nicole, the phone rang.

"Ignore it," Bernard caressed her breast. "They can call tomorrow. Right now, you are all mine. I want to touch you. I want you to know what it's like being with me."

"Oh Bernard," she feigned excitement.

"That's right baby. I want to taste you over and over again. First, I want to make you call out my name then I want you to suck me dry." His hands were already on his pants.

The machine clicked on. Billy's voice filled the room. "Hey baby. I want to do something special for you tonight to work on us. I'll be over in about fifteen minutes. See you then."

Nicole looked at Bernard with the same surprised look he gave her. They spoke at the same time. "I think you should go."

"I think I should go."

Quickly, Bernard picked up his things while Nicole cleaned the kitchen. With a quick kiss he was gone.

Billy waited ten minutes then came out of the guest closet.

"That was an uncomfortable and close one."

Nicole sighed, "Yes, but we have accomplished much up to this point."

"Every time I see him touch you, I want to kill him. This time he saw you half naked."

"Honey, don't start now. In order to break the man's heart, he has to be fully in love or think that he somehow possesses me. Then when I leave, he'll be worse than ever. Of course, not before he realizes we're getting married and is embarrassed before the entire town of Scarborough." Nicole gave an imitation evil laugh.

Billy smiled, "Babe, you're something special."

"And you are worth it to me. Just wait."

Tuesday night after class, just as Nicole was leaving, a voice came out of the night. "Just what do you think you're doing?"

The voice of Shannon Enlow scared a preoccupied Nicole. The willowy blonde emerged from the shadows.

"Going home?"

"Spare me. I know you're going out with Bernard. Girlfriend, take another route."

"I know what I'm doing."

"Sure you do. Does this mean Billy is available?"

"Hell no!" slipped out before Nicole knew it.

"Now, that doesn't sound like a woman who 'knows what she's doing'." The last words were punctuated.

Nicole opened the door of her car. Shannon

quickly shut it. She eyed the other blond suspiciously, "Just what are you doing?"

"Testing the waters. Now if you will kindly move." She got in her car.

This time Shannon held the door open. "Look, I think you are a good person. You are too good for the likes of him. You were one of the few people that chose to remain speaking to me after all those rumors got started. I don't want to see anyone go through the things I went through. I'm just trying to tell you. Do you want to end up like me?"

"I won't. Trust me."

"If I can't change your mind, you can call me if you need me," Shannon said as she gave the other woman a worried look.

"Don't worry. Everything is under control."

"TJ, my friend." The voice on the other end of the phone was none other than Bernard.

"Hey *pedrone*, my favorite customer, friend

and *sensei*. How's it hanging?"

"Good man. You sound high."

"Would I be any other way?" Both men laughed. "Knowing you're all business, what can I do for you?"

"Need a camera man. Doing a show I want professionally done."

"Anybody I know?"

"Nicole."

"Oh man!" TJ took a drag on his blunt. "Can I join?"

"Maybe. Depends how far she will let me go after we have been together a few months. Maybe a little double time."

"Good looking out." TJ felt himself getting stiff.

"Man, do you know how long I've been waiting for that hot ass?"

"Hell yeah. Years. You scored yet?"

"No, but I'm on second base."

"Sweet. When?"

"Now, there's a problem. I keep pushing, she keeps running. A few months at the most."

"Why not use your heavenly mix? Guaranteed score."

"That would ruin it. Man, I'll let you know. We can use the equipment at the house. I'll need your lights."

TJ whistled, "You *are* going for quality."

"If she's prime goods, I've got to keep her hanging on. If I am lucky, she might catch some feelings."

"True. Hey man while I got you; I got some new flicks in."

"What about?"

"Preeny Teenies, Red Clan and some guerrilla footage from the net."

Bernard's stiffened at the thought of TJ's selections. Preeny Teenies was quality stuff. He never knew how the producer got those ten and twelve year old girls to have sex with anything from teenage boys to six grown men; but he

liked it. Red Clan videos were imported from
China. They were normally sex torture of
prisoners or enemies of the state. He was not
sure about the last item. As much as he liked
S&M and forcible intercourse, sometimes the
tape quality was poor. The more he thought of
those ten year old preteens being banged from
behind, the harder he got.

"Yo B man, you still there?"

"Yeah, yeah. I'll take them all. Look, I need
them tonight. I'll call Amanda and swing in the
back of the shop for this new stash."

"You still hitting that?"

"Oh yeah. Nicole's not in my bed yet. Plus,
you know we got her show coming up in two
weeks. She's acting funny lately. Wanting me
to eat and treat her all nice. She must think I'm
a butch or something." Bernard rolled his eyes,
reflecting on the last time she was at the house.
She was almost annoying. She didn't want him
in her mouth or ass. Like she didn't know the
usual routine.

"Whatever. What time?"

"Hour."

"Cash in hand. Later."

"Later."

TJ hung up the phone, his high leaving. Bernard was a great customer, but he hated working for him at times. Especially when it involved the people in the karate school, people he looked at every week. Nicole was a bitch, but she was all business when it came to karate. He respected her skill and knowledge but would not mind hitting that ass just once. Bernard was going to make that possible. Amanda was a different story. The jury was still out on her. She seemed nice and polite enough, but always steered clear of him, like he was dirty or something. That was Bernard's flavor of the month. He went to brush his teeth as if the taste of the blunt or talking to Bernard left a bad taste in his mouth.

Si

Weeks had passed since Nicole talked with Shannon. Since then, she had seen Bernard routinely twice a week. She started going out of town on weekends to avoid seeing him. Billy cut down on coming to class. He was distant and brooding when there. Bernard was his usual self, as usual goes. Flirting with women, taking frustrations out on the class, looking for new women to score, treating the old women he had already used with no respect. Everyday Bernard.

One weekend, Nicole did stay. Bernard insisted on coming over. The extra time together would not hurt, so she agreed. After they picnicked, he wanted to go back to his place. He was driving, so she did not have a choice. This was her first mistake. He told her he only wanted to feed the dogs. Once that was over, he came up behind her and began kissing her. He tried to lead her to his study, but Nicole knew better. She suggested the living room and he settled.

Once there he began again, this time more physical than in the kitchen. His groping was rough and his kisses less playful. She needed an out. She and Billy had discussed what would happen if she would go all the way. She was not ready yet. Her out came in the haunting form of his dead wife. She looked up to see Rita's wedding portrait over the mantle. Nicole said a mental thank you to the person in the picture then stiffened up. "Bernard."

"What?"

"I can't do this."

"WHAT!" He sat up.

"Not here."

"I said the study."

Nicole shook her head, "Not in this room, not in your study and not in this house. Her home."

"Her?" His face frowned then changed to surprise. "Oh you mean Rita. Well, she's gone. She won't mind, she would want me to be happy."

"I mind. Can't we just go to my house?"

Bernard pouted, "But we're already here."

"Yes, here, as in her house. Besides here doesn't have black lacy cup-less things, does it?" she winked.

"No. Cup-less, uh. All right, we'll go to your house only if you promise to make it good.

"Deal."

On the way to her place, Nicole's mind raced to put the necessary pieces in place. She had never done anything without Billy as a backup. She made the excuse of having to check her messages, but first got him a beer. She came back from the kitchen saying she was out of his usual favorite but had some new beer. After the first swallow, he made a face. She insisted he reserve judgment until he finished the beer. Then, she checked her messages while watching him drink. She pretended to make two calls; one to Billy and one to her service. She offered him another beer. He gladly accepted. She returned with his beer. He captured her hand and said, "Now, what about that something black and lacy?"

She smiled weakly, "Okay, I'll be right back."

She took her time finding a black negligee with robe. She walked out to show Bernard. His mouth dropped open. He swallowed hard and rose to go to her.

"Wait," she had an instant idea. He gave her an angry puzzled look. "I want this to be a little show. I have more."

Bernard grinned and sat back down, "I like that one, but I hope it gets better."

Nicole disappeared into her bedroom again. When she came out in a white lace negligee, Bernard had his shirt off. She walked in front of him and modeled.

"Nice," he said rubbing his growing erection.

"One last one. Please put your shirt on. It takes away from undressing you."

He complied as she exited the room. Nicole had stalled enough. As she slipped on the red outfit, she checked the time. She had saved the best for last. She walked out in an outfit that made Bernard swear loudly. She stood over him in a red leather outfit, complete with red teddy underneath, red thigh high boots and garter belt attached to fish net stockings.

"You like?"

"Hell Yes!" He pulled her down on the couch. His hands were shaking as he unzipped her jacket. "I always imagined you like this, sexy as hell and wanting me."

"Let me undress you first." Bernard obeyed. She had blown his mind with her outfit. He was putty in her hands now. With extra slowness and sensuality, she took off his clothes, leaving nothing but boxer briefs.

Next, it was his turn. First her boots. He sucked her toes through fishnet hose. Next her jacket. He sloppily kissed her between movements. His hand pinched and kneaded her flesh. He unzipped her skirt and removed it. He stood over her looking down.

"What's wrong?"

"Nothing. I just wanted to savor the sight of you."

"How about savoring the sight in the bedroom. Carry me."

A little unsteady, but wanting to show he was still in control, Bernard carried her to her bedroom. Once on the bed, he removed his boxers. Nicole had no idea how well endowed he was. If she had to do this, she would at least enjoy it. He stood beside the bed, rubbing his already erect member. "Suck it."

"What?"

He repeated, "Suck it. Put it in your mouth and suck it."

"You first."

"Not yet."

She looked at him. He was swaying. "I've never done this before."

Bernard snorted with disbelief, "Well baby, there's a first time for everything. Just put it in your mouth and try."

She was timid, so he positioned her sitting on the edge of the bed so that she had to bend over to attend to requested task. His hand moved in her hair and guided her inches from his erection. Feeling trapped, she opened her mouth. He was gentle at first. Slowly moving her head back and forth. Nicole thought if this was all she had to do, it might be okay. Then, Bernard got vigorous, pushing her head down while his hips trust forward at the same time. Nicole was so caught off guard she grabbed his thighs to keep her balance. She had no idea his thighs were so tight and tone. She began choking but he continued. She bit down and Bernard pushed her away. Irritated he said, "The one rule in giving head is no teeth."

"I said I didn't know how," she flung back.

"You're right," he slid on the bed in front of her. "I did say try. Not bad for your first time. You'll get better."

"And how are your skills?"

His answer was to push her back. He kissed her while his hands worked at her teddy. He peeled down the top of her teddy so her oversized breast could spring free. He did a little work on them, tasting her peaks and the valley between them. He was not a chest man. He removed the teddy leaving only fish net pantyhose. Without a pause, he parted her legs and went to work. Nicole knew she was not supposed to enjoy this but he was good. His tongue was like silk on bare skin. Over and over again he made her climax. In the midst of one of many senseless orgasms, he grabbed her wrist and slipped in. Nicole felt him and protested. He seemed drugged and did not acknowledge her. He began trusting hard, making her wiggle with pleasure. The good sex was clouding her judgment. She climaxed again before she noticed his thrust were getting slower. She insisted he go down between her thighs again. Tired, he did as he was told. His tongue was less magic this time. In moments it stopped altogether.

"Bernard?"

He was out. She rolled him over on the bed. That was a close one that went way further than she planned. She would never tell Billy about this. She thought everything was fine until she saw his erection. Dammit! Nicole knew he needed to release to believe they had sex. Acting quickly, she found a bottle of baby lotion and jacked him off. She made sure his semen got on her chest and chin. His stickiness made her vomit a little in her mouth. To make it look authentic, she rubbed some semen on her thighs. Just like the movies. She waited to see if he would wake up. She leaned over and began whispering in his ear. After an hour of feeling unnecessarily sticky, she dozed off.

When she woke up, she was cold. Then Nicole remembered, she was naked. The clocked reported 4:40 am. She went to the bathroom for a shower. The shower must have awakened Bernard. He was sitting up slowly. She watched amused as he tried to get his bearings. He looked from her teddy on the floor to her standing in the door comically. He smiled a little unsure.

She waited.

He got off the bed shakily and walked over to her. He was a beautiful sight for a sixty plus year old man. Broad shoulders, a four instead of six pack, track thighs and an impressive male member even when it was limp. He kissed her while rubbing himself against her torso. She could fell him growing stiff and put a stop to his activity. "Oh no."

"No?"

"Not after last night."

He was genuinely puzzled, "What didn't you like about last night that I don't really remember, um, much?"

"Well let's see; I thought you would have done a little better for our first time than just slamming me from behind. Then there was the trying to screw me in the ass. When I said no, you went back to extra hard doggie. Bernard, I have bruises that I may have to explain to Billy. Remember I haven't told him about us yet."

"I'm sorry. Next time I'll be gentle. It's just I can't get off by treating a woman like she's glass during sex. A real man takes a woman anyway he can. He makes her sore so she can remember who made her feel that way for days afterward," he offered. "Also, I was drinking. Wine and that damn beer just didn't mix well for me."

"You can say that again. But that was not an excuse for coming in my face."

"Next time it will be better," he lied.

"You're damn right. Next time it will be my way or no way. Now get dressed and go home. Billy might be on his way over here with breakfast or something," she was dismissing him.

"When is next time?"

"Whenever the soreness and bruises go away. We can still go out, just give me a week or two. I want to, no need to officially call it quits with Billy."

Bernard smiled. Good enough. He had some things to do anyway. "All right. Until next time."

She kissed him, "See you in class Tuesday."

"Tuesday."

The things Bernard had to do were with Amanda. Lately, she was changing and he had to let her know what time it was, that he was and would always be in control. Once a woman was with him, they belonged to him. In addition, he had to make sure no matter what happened, she would always be in his available ass collection.

For a week, he wined and dined her. He fit Nicole in on Wednesday and Friday. He was an uncharacteristic angel with both women. He did not push Nicole past her limit. They went out and he only went back to her house once. He fell asleep during a movie they had rented, kissed her and went home.

Go

For Amanda, he was the Bernard of old. On nights they were together, he controlled his urges and made slow love to her instead. This pleased Amanda to no end. She even suggested an experimental threesome. The idea turned him on slightly. He had had several, but not with her. She wanted another female. His answer was that he would think about it.

Next week, Nicole missed Tuesday due to an out of town matter. He was disappointed, but was surprised when she called him at the office. He wanted to see her Thursday after class. She said she would be gone the rest of the week. This gave Bernard the opportunity of setting up Amanda.

TJ was in class Thursday. Bernard gave him a key. Saturday night, he was to be in the study, ready to go by 10pm. Bernard did not see Amanda until Saturday. They went to an early show and late dinner. He brought her back to the house. They played on the internet looking at various porn sites. After her second beer, the drugs had Amanda beyond drunk, he made sure of that. Bernard saw this coming and led her into the study.

He sat her in his chair, while TJ turned on the lights. He was ready as Bernard undressed a drugged Amanda. He did this with such agonizing slowness; the average layman might think this was the beginning of a love making session. With Amanda completely naked and some what semi-conscious, Bernard sat on the edge of his desk facing her. He took out his erection and put it in her mouth. With her mouth being slack, he moved her head with a rhythm he liked. Her gagging reflex made him go faster. When they came more frequent, he stopped. He had a long night ahead and did not need her sick. Instead, he spoke softly to her.

"Amanda, dear, do you love me?"

She looked blankly ahead.

"I know you do. Tonight, I'm going to give you the threesome you asked for. I'm going to start. Now over the desk with you." He pulled her up and bent her over the desk. Without a hitch, he stuck his rock hard member in her ass and pumped away.

TJ looked through the lens, holding the camera with one hand while the other stroked his genitals.

Bernard withdrew so he could bite her on the ass. He turned her over and positioned her knees around his waist and drilled her ass again, for a different on camera look. Her tight ass was making him want to come. Impaled on him, he picked her up with ease. He moved over to the settee where he asked TJ to join them. He stopped rubbing his growing erection long enough to set the camera on a tripod.

Turning Amanda on her stomach on the settee, Bernard returned to his vigorous stroking rhythm in her ass when TJ stuffed himself in and out of her mouth. With a hail of curses, Bernard finished in her ass. While he went to the bathroom, TJ's frustration in his current position grew. The bitch was not sucking him; he was fucking a slack mouth. No sooner than Bernard left, than TJ slipped on a condom, looped her legs around his neck and drove into her dripping wet sex. Damn her shit was tight! TJ wondered what she was like when she was not drugged into a mindless sex plaything. She was moaning and feebly attempted to resist him. This excited him to the point that he grabbed her breast, leaving scratch marks. She made him almost forget the camera. He pumped in her a few more times, then released on her chest for cinematic effect. Now, he really needed a blunt. He left Amanda the zombie sprawled on the settee.

Bernard came back, ready again. This time he brought toys. He handcuffed Amanda to a hidden bar under the eve of his desk. She moaned in weak resistance. The drug could only last so long. He posed her laying on her stomach across his desk. He strapped on the black shiny dildo right above his own erection. Bernard positioned her ass up so the camera could get the shot. He slipped the dildo in her ass and his own in her other waiting wetness. The juices from her ass ran down on his in motion member, heightening his excitement. He began slapping her ass. He must haven gotten carried away because she began to make whiny noises. This angered Bernard. He reached over and slapped her head.

"You shut your mouth bitch! You know you

like this shit."

Tears ran down her face. Bernard stopped and stomped to the closet frustrated. He came from the closet with her punishment. He attached a leather band around her throat and held the other end in his hand. He resumed his previous position, this time showing no mercy. Whenever she whined or cried out, he would pull on the leather leash causing her to choke. After a while, he just pulled on the leash because her choke exited him more.

The door opened quietly. Both men looked at Clay Kennedy. Clay looked from his uncle to TJ to Amanda. Time seemed frozen. Bernard recovered from his shock with a smile, "I don't know what you are doing here, but either join in or get out."

It only took Clay a second to remember how Amanda had dumped him for his purse string uncle. Clay crossed the room and stood on the corner of the desk. He unzipped his pants and thus emerged his semi hard member. Amanda tried to move but she was trapped. Her right arm was handcuffed to the desk and Bernard was behind her. Bernard pulled on her leash and barked orders for her to suck his nephew. She obeyed him and took Clay in her mouth.

"Suck it bitch! Bernard! She's not doing anything."

"Amanda, suck or choke."

She did as told, but she could not keep the tears from staining his pants.

"Shit! None of that." Clay took his pants off and propped one kneed on the desk. "Lick my balls now."

Amanda did as commanded. Bernard worked himself into a frenzy. Both toy and man going at the same time was ecstasy. She came squirting Bernard. She would have cried out if not for Clay in her mouth. His hands making her go down over and over again.

Then Clay and Bernard switched, pausing only to cuff her hands behind her back and put her over the settee. The fog in her brain was ebbing. Amanda could not believe Bernard would do this to her. Her thoughts were punctuated by Bernard opening her mouth and sticking himself in, "Come on baby. You've done this before."

She did as she was told, remembering the leash. What she forgot was Clay, until he slipped in from behind. The only thing she could do was cry. After forever, she felt Clay's wet hot load. He slumped over her only momentarily. She turned her attention to Bernard. If she could get him off, this would be over. As usual, he came in her mouth, making her swallow.

Her body relaxed. That might have been the beginning of her nightmare. Bernard said, "Remember your wish for a threesome. Now you'll get it and more."

TJ had an idea what Bernard meant when he sat on the settee and pulled Amanda onto his lap entering her ass from behind. Then he lay back, pulling her with him. She looked impaled. TJ did not need another hint. He put out his blunt and placed the camera on the tripod. He checked the shot, slipped on another condom and straddled them both to get in her wet swollen sex. When she cried loudly, Bernard called to Clay. He came from the desk, put himself in her mouth again. The trio worked as synchronized as they could. TJ came first, snatching off the condom to spray her chest. He picked up the camera and moved around for angles. He told Clay to jack off in her face. His semen and her tears ran on Bernard. With Clay gone, Bernard sat up and bounced her up and down until she came in spite of herself. When he came, he made sure it looked good for the camera.

Bernard got up to get her a chair. She offered no resistance as she was either tired, drugged or escaped to a corner in her own mind. He turned on the TV to show the guys his last film. One of the college students was being ravaged over his desk. She was gagged and bar cuffed. While they watched, Bernard bathed Amanda. He did it carefully and slowly. He massaged her shoulders while assuring her that he giving her wishes and wildest fantasy. He traded the handcuffs for two purple scarves. With one he tied her hands together, and the other around his neck. He put her on the couch between Clay and TJ. He knelt in front of her and buried his face between her legs. As the three of them watched Bernard on the TV, he used his tongue to make Amanda climax to multiple organism. When her head was spinning from pleasure, he blindfolded her with the other scarf and laid her down on the couch.

Amanda did not know what was happening until she felt someone on top of her, parting her legs. She could not see who it was. First the person was missionary, then doggie style in the ass. She called Bernard's name several times, but he did not answer. She felt that person's hot seed spray her back. With that over, she wanted to relax, but seconds later a fresh erection slid in with the new person putting her on the floor on her shoulders. That did not seem to satisfy him, so it was back to missionary. The pounding came to a stop with loud grunts and hot semen spilling out of her. Without a hitch, a new hard erection took the place of the removed shrinking one. This one was familiar. She knew it was Bernard because he came in her mouth.

This went on twice more before the men were tired and Amanda was destroyed. Afterward, she lay huddled on the couch, fluids running out of every orifice. Amanda did not know how much time passed. She dragged herself to the bathroom and threw up. She found her towel and took a shower. She stayed under the water until it ran ice cold. Without a second thought, she walked out of the bathroom and began trying to dial 911.

A sleepy voice answered hello.

Amanda just broke down crying, trying to tell someone she was raped.

"Whoa! Slow down."

"No I can't! I need help! Please!"

"Who is this?"

"Amanda Dunneski."

There was a sharp intake on the other end. "Amanda, this is Barbara from karate. This is not 911. You must have hit the memory button. Look, stay where you are. I'll be right there. Don't move. I'll be right there."

In less than half an hour, Barbara was there with Rocky. Quickly, they collected her and went to Barbara's house. Barbara called Nicole's answering service. Amanda was showering again when she called back. Barbara gave her a brief rundown for advice. Nicole suggested an ER visit. Barbara was convinced the girl would not go for that. Nicole then thought it best to watch her for the night. Given the grim details, anything could happen from internal bleeding to suicide attempts. Nicole would be back in town tomorrow afternoon to assist from there.

After hanging up, Barbara relayed the information to Rocky. When Amanda came out of the shower, they convinced her to stay there the night. She reluctantly agreed, but wanted to make a call. Rocky went home, but Barbara and Amanda stayed up talking until the sun came up. Barbara made breakfast then both women finally got some much needed sleep.

The call from Nicole stirred them early evening. She had an idea and was on the way over. Once there she explained that they would visit the emergency room with complaint of lower abdominal pains. Nicole would accompany her to fend off any questions. They would call Barbara from the hospital. Amanda agreed to this on one condition: that Shannon met them there. With a puzzled glance at Barbara, Nicole consented. Plan in place, they were off to University Road to the hospital.

Amanda filled out the paperwork while Nicole talked to the triage nurse. Shannon arrived before she went in the back for her exam. Her presence seemed to sooth, yet unravel Amanda. She cried for several minutes.

Nicole tried not to notice, but the girl kept saying 'you said not to trust him' and 'I was trying to leave him'. Shannon took her to the bathroom. When they came out, Amanda was calmer. She was called back and both women went as well.

Amanda got through the initial questions, repeating what Nicole told her to say. She became unnerved when she was asked to undress. Somehow Shannon got her through that and the pelvic exam. The attending physician could not help but look at the bruises and scratches then at Nicole, who frowned. She left the room to recompose. The thought of Bernard and whoever did this was just too much. Nicole was wiping tears when the doctor came out. He gave her a moment then said, "I suppose there is no chance this could be a rape case."

"I really don't know. With her it might have been consensual. Some like it rough."

"But why come here?"

"Maybe things got too rough."

"Should I suggest the rape kit?"

"Why? She took a few showers over the last few hours. It was probably her lover and that would bring the police into their sex life. I'm sure after this little incident it won't be long before their relationship will be over."

Before walking away the doctor said, "I hope so. An ER visit would do the trick for me."

Shannon came out fuming, "How in the hell did this happen?"

"I have no clue. Barbara called me."

"I'll kill that bastard," she paused, "I thought he was your man now. How could you let him do this?"

"First, he's not my man and second, you know yourself, Bernard cannot be controlled. But while that may be the issue, there's another something here that you have not come out and said."

"Maybe."

Nicole rolled her eyes. "Please. Everybody here is not as naive as Amanda. Regardless, after this, it won't happen again."

"How can you be so sure?"

"I can't right now. What we can do is take care of Amanda. You take her home. I'll be in touch." Nicole walked in the room to say her farewells.

Roku

Amanda had not been to class since her incident, but Shannon urged her to face Bernard. Shannon called his office and talked with Barbara. Though reluctant at first, Barbara agreed it should be done. She set a meeting at a super public place: the food court at the mall. Shannon would wait in a nearby store.

Amanda was jumpy as a cat. She jumped when he sat down.

"Amanda, darling where have you been? You don't return any of my calls."

She did not respond at first.

"Amanda?" He tried to hold her hand.

"No. Don't." She let out a heavy sigh, "Don't you think you have done enough touching me?"

"What? Surely you don't mean the last time we were together. I gave you what you wanted," he sounded truly incredulous.

A half laugh escaped Amanda. "What I wanted? What I wanted was just you, the romantic fun you. What I got was . . . was," her voice faltered. "You tell me what I was supposed to get, what I am suppose to think. Because all I have is nightmares of something gone horribly wrong. That night comes back to me in flashes. Every flash of memories is accompanied by pain, shame and always hurt. I TRUSTED YOU! I loved you and I thought you loved me. You don't know what it feels like to have the person you love have you perform like a circus whore."

Silent tears streamed down her face.

"Amanda, I'm sorry you feel this way. This was not my intent. I only thought to please you. To give us something to add to our bedroom. You liked the videos. We watched them before. We talked about making one. I even called you the next day. Then you just disappeared. When was I ever going to see you and talk about this? You even withdrew from school. Look, I want to fix this misunderstanding." He leaned toward her.

This time she leveled him with a look filled with contempt and seething hatred. "Misunderstanding! Misunderstanding? Is that what you call giving me some drug and recording me having sex with three men at the same time? You forced me to have sex with your own nephew, TJ from the karate class, and whoever else you brought in while I was blinded and helpless."

"A misunderstanding," she spat out "Is that what you call what wakes me up at night and leaves me in the fetal position; the same position you left me in that night? Is that what you call these anxiety attacks, this inability to trust any man within three feet of me or the fact when I put on a blindfold now I pass out? Or is the misunderstanding that twice a year for the rest of my life I am going to get a blood test for an incurable disease."

"I don't have AIDS."

"How about Clay and TJ or the other men you had come join in? You know, my unseen, unknown assailants. Well don't misunderstand this: if I could I would take you to court, but I have been advised not to. But if you ever come near me again, I will kill you and happily spend my four years locked up in a mental hospital. Hell, I'm already in a mental jail cell, locked up there thanks to you." She got up and left the table.

For one of the few times of his life, Bernard was speechless. He did not know what shocked him the most, the fact she reacted the way she did, that she left him, or that she threatened to kill him and meant it. THAT BITCH! He would have to go home and watch the video again just to make sure he treated her like the bitch she was. He would jack off to her shame and humiliation again and again.

On upside of it all, he was done with her for now and that could focus on keeping Nicole as his main thing and adding Vanessa or one of those new girls from campus as his new side thing. He lived to break bitches like her: snobby and aloof. They all cried and were reduced to common bitches in heat like a dog on the street covered in his semen. And always on video for his later pleasure to re-live the moment as much as he liked. He was going after her when he got tired of Amanda anyway. Much as he liked Nicole in his bed, the thought of someone exotic as Vanessa reduced to nothing on camera was what he really wanted.

He must have been thinking about her too hard because he almost thought he saw her walking past him to the mall food court. Looking again, blinking as if to clear his vision, he saw it was her and she was not alone. Drew was her lunch date. They were laughing and kissing. Disgusted and unable to handle anymore shock today, Bernard collected himself and walked out the mall, not even noticing Shannon standing twenty feet away reporting the whole scenario on the cell phone.

Drew missed class Tuesday night, so Bernard made it a point to stop by after kick boxing class on Wednesday. After checking most of the *dojo*, he came to talk with Drew.

"*Sensei*, I didn't know you were coming by."

"Well, you missed class last night. What's going on?"

"Nothing. I just had a few things to do last night." Drew started to get defensive.

"Things or people?" Bernard snapped back.

"Maybe both. Look what's this really all about? You don't ever give other folks this much grief over one class. Especially not the females. Especially not Nicole." Drew threw out a barb.

"I don't want you bringing down one of my rising students." Bernard never heard Barbara walking out of the locker room. She was catching a ride home with Drew. "I know you have a thing for Vanessa. She has the potential to reach first rank or second rank. Missing class will hold her back."

"B, I don't encourage Vanessa to skip class. She's grown and so am I. I don't know what this is really about, but you are over the line," Drew hedged out.

"I'm saying let her be with her kind and you with yours." Bernard shrugged, "I know your mother would not have wanted you dating anything but a black woman."

"Don't you bring my mother into this!" Drew squared up with Bernard, "My mother would have wanted me to be happy. I know she would have slapped you stupid had she been here to hear your speech. The two of you grew up together. She stood by you through whatever and regardless of race. Now you come in here all klansman on me because you don't approve of who I date. This conversation is over; so if you want to lockup you can, but I promised Rocky I would."

"You just remember what I said," Bernard shot back as he turned to leave.

"Whatever," Drew said to his back. "She won't be your flavor of the month. Doc ain't giving up that spot."

When he was gone, Barbara stepped out of the office shaking her head. "Of all the years I've known him, he's never sounded like that."

"Mom said he was a sweetheart until you got in his way."

"I've worked with Bernard in that office and in karate and I never knew he wanted Vanessa."

"Yeah, I thought he was all about Nicole and Amanda."

Barbara glanced around. "I don't think Amanda will be coming back."

"I noticed she hasn't been here. Shame, because she was really sweet."

"Bernard can corrupt the best of the best. I should know."

Drew looked slapped, "Not you and B."

"No, not like that. Plus, if you sleep with your conscience, then who will guide you down the right path? No, I was never even attracted to Bernard. Probably because when I met him, I was married. Curtis and I moved here from Georgia. My boys were eleven, ten and five and my husband's new love was kickboxing. Two nights a week, he would drive from Rain Hills to train with Bernard. Bernard was a local celebrity and famed champion, thinking about training others. At first it was just a few guys working with a retired kickboxer."

"My first introduction was at one of his matches in Andover. Bernard invited Curt. I was so impressed with his intensity and natural athleticism; I wished Curt were that way. I was pleased when their friendship blossomed. Bernard had divorced Sherry by then and I had a good relationship with B. He and I could talk or do things without Curtis. He and Curtis started training daily. They were inseparable and traveled at least once a month. Vegas, Little Rock, Mexico City, Manhattan, you name it. The extra money we got from the fights was a huge help to the household. Between the military, my school loans and the fights, we purchased a home in the country, which is now Sumnerville, got me reliable transportation and my husband, a luxury car. We were fine for years. So, I did not see my husband leaving me for the sister of another fighter."

"Curt was obviously planning ahead because he emptied our stocks and bank account. I was devastated. I was a stay at home mom going to college with three boys. To put it plainly, I blamed Bernard. Curt was his best friend; how could Bernard not have known that he was going to leave his family. Either out of guilt or genuine concern Bernard stepped right in. He paid my tuition, gave me money for the boys and a part time job in his office. When I finished school, I went to work full time out of obligation. We were close, so he felt comfortable confiding in me as his perversions grew."

"I don't know if Sherry's leaving hurt him that bad, but he became a twisted sexual predator. He went through girlfriends like water. I learned what was going on when one of the girls came to the office totally belligerent. She was ranting about sex toys and videos. When I got her out of the office, in a quiet spot, she told me about a night I had heard about numerous times since then. When I confronted Bernard about that particular girl, he dismissed the incident as a disgruntled girlfriend, relationship gone wrong, psycho-bitch, anything but what it actually was."

"I approached Bernard twice more, once after this pretty little girl from Dayspring and second after Shannon. The first time he agreed to go to therapy; he knew he needed help. With Shannon, he blew it off, made it seem like something she wanted. That is his very feeling to this day. Somehow in his mind, he believes that the women he's with should willingly participate and accept his behavior. If she doesn't like a certain thing, she should expect him to push the limit until she comes into his line of thinking. Bitches, is what he calls them. Common bitches that want him to do them like dogs in the street," Barbara finished quietly.

Drew seemed speechless. He finally

manages to utter an "I can't believe this." Then he asked, "Did my mother know all this?"

Barbara shrugged, "Probably not. Would you tell your sister, even if she was someone you valued more than your own sister, what you were doing in your bedroom?"

"All these years, my mom thought B was so great. One of the best things in her life, even named him my godfather. If she only knew." Drew shook his head.

Barbara put a hand on his shoulder, "Drew, thank God for two things. One that your mom never knew and two that Vanessa has you. Come on let's lock up this place and save Bernard for another class day."

"You know Nicole, you have a problem." Shannon was on the other end of Nicole's phone.

Nicole sighed, "What is it Shannon and why is it a problem?"

"The last few days I followed you. I was not pressed about Bernard, but I was confused and concerned when I saw Billy around you. I think B would be too, knowing him as I do. If you're playing him, he will make your life miserable. You've already seen first hand what he can do. You know you can't tease him forever. Bernard will get more aggressive each time. He'll become frustrated and overpowering with you. If his aggression and frustration builds, he might take you by force like he did Amanda."

Nicole chewed her lip. "I'll talk to Billy. Meet me in Watly on Sunday at 1:00 pm. If I don't have an answer to your proposed dilemma, we can work something out."

"Watly?"

"My spot or nothing. You can tell Bernard that you think he's being played if you like, but we both know what's between my thighs is worth a thousand words." Nicole shot back.

"If only you knew. If that's what you think of B, you're in for a rude awakening."

"How's Amanda?"

"Withdrawn. Traumatized. Coping. She

might have to take incompletes this semester."

"We could go shopping afterward and maybe buy Amanda something nice." Nicole hung up, mind racing.

The week passed as usual. After Tuesday night at Nicole's, she fended Bernard off again by promising an office visit the next day. Long before Wednesday and unbeknownst to Billy, Nicole decided it was time to escalate things a bit to keep gaining Bernard's trust. The more time she spent with him, the more curious she became. What kept her in constant check was flashbacks of Amanda. Seeing that girl in the hospital never left her mind. Considering she was always two steps ahead of Bernard, the office visit was a must. Dressed in a garter belt, stockings and an orange and white wrap dress without a bra, Nicole felt vexed with each step heading toward his office. She felt like her body was a traitor and hated that her mind slipped to the last time they had physical contact. Breezing past the partner's secretaries, Nicole noticed Barbara's office empty. She poked her head in the door, "Where's Barb?"

"Getting a spa treatment on me." Bernard

pulled her in and locked the doors behind them. He kissed her while pressing his hardness between her legs. Nicole let him discover her surprises. His hand pushed up her dress. "God, you are so wet! I need to see it. I need to feel you, taste you and whatever else pleases me."

With a pull on her bow, she stood before him in only garter belt, stockings and pumps. Bernard licked his suddenly dry lips, "You look good enough to eat."

Positioning her on his desk, Bernard put all Nicole's lovers past and present to shame. She was so caught up that her moans escalated to guttural grunts. Her sexual fluids stained the floor. As she was half crazy from pleasure, he slipped right in. He was so good. His nine inch erection caused her own sex to contract as she moaned. The more her muscles convulsed and constricted the better he got. She felt him getting faster. He urged her to climax with him. "Wait!"

"What!"

"Wait. I-I've got something to show you."

"Honey, it can't get much better than this. I

want to shoot off in your mouth. I want you to swallow me. Every drop."

"Sit in your chair." He obliged, rock hard erection between them like a pole.

She went down on him, taking as much of him in her mouth as she could. Her hand, glided by her own wetness, and her mouth gave his head a fit. Billy never let her be this freaky but Bernard lived for it. He encouraged her. "Oh yes baby!! Suck me off. Damn you got better in a hurry."

Nothing a dozen porn movies and a few sex books could not fix.

She stopped and eased on him just enough for rim shots on the tip of his erection. Bernard went nuts, squeezing her breast until they hurt. She would rim his erection a minute then go back to suck him while gripping his shaft. Back to rimming his head then taking him in her mouth.

"Damn baby!" His legs shook.

"Not yet. One more thing."

"Better that this?"

"Rock my boat and spray on my face."

"What?" Bernard seemed confused.

Nicole laid down on her side on his desk with one leg between his and one on his shoulder. "Now do my clit just like you were inside me. Slide it in for that extra wetness."

Though awkward at first he got the hang of it. He pumped in her wet tight sex muscles then grinded against her hard clit. His whole desk was covered in slick stickiness as she succumbed to multiple orgasms. Nicole seemed to be running out of energy. She had to finish her way or it would be his for sure. Weakly, she turned on her back and pushed her breast up to lick her own nipples.

Needing no more of an invitation, Bernard pushed then pinned her arms to her sides by positioned himself swatting on her stomach. He smiled in this power position as he rubbed her own juices on her breast for extra lubrication then molded her 36Ds around his hurting erection. Nicole lifted her head so she could taste him. Her mouth proved no match for his continuous thrust. He shoved her head back and worked her breast without mercy. With a bellow that Nicole was sure the whole building heard, Bernard exploded over her face, neck and chest. His limbs seemed electrocuted. He slid off her chest and back in her wet sex where his incessant jerking and his palm against her clit made her climax again.

Nicole floated somewhere between guilt and ecstasy. Never was sex so freakishly spectacular. If Billy ever found out, she was very dead. Stupid behavior could ruin everything. Bernard jarred her thoughts by saying, "Where did that come from and why couldn't you do that at home?

"We should have been home. All of your office heard us."

"My office is sound proof. I can shoot a gun and nobody would hear. Trust me. I think my nuts were as loud as yours."

"Nuts?"

"Baby, I couldn't control myself. Your body was hot for that clit thing, but for me to keep it going I needed to be inside you. I came and kept going. That coming on your tits and face thing was my dream come true."

"Bernard, didn't I tell you I have not started my birth control," Nicole lied. "Are you trying to get me pregnant?"

Walking toward his private bathroom he threw a washcloth and the question, "Would that be so bad? You could leave Billy and do me everyday. Be my love slave and mother to my child."

Siti

Love slave. Slave. Like Amanda. That whole conversation and the consequences played in her head on the way to Watly on Sunday. On the way to the outlet, Nicole gave Shannon sketchy details of her intent, leaving out events on Wednesday.

"It won't work."

"Why?"

"Because to get closer to B, you're going to have to sex him dirty. Then he'll really let his guard down."

"Billy said no. He'll abandon this thing first."

"That's the only way. I know from experience. You now, I wasn't always this way. When I came here, I transferred from a community college in my hometown. I lived home all my life and came here knowing nothing. I never had a serious relationship until

I got to the university. I had only been with one guy. I became popular when I joined the dance team. Bernard came to our physical conditioning to give pointers on flexibility and endurance. He invited us to the karate school a few times. He would make it a point to see me during sponsored socials."

"Can you imagine how a twenty year old felt being pursued by an older rich gentleman? Flowers, office parties, weekends away. He wasn't married to Rita then. It all partying and travel definitely effected my grades. I lost my eligibility and he just took care of everything. And he wanted me to dance for him. We had only petted heavily for months, so when he said I could just do my routine, I agreed. Soon enough, he asked me to make my dancing more risqué. I was okay with doing that because I wanted so hard to please him and show him my appreciation for all he had done for me. One night, there was a storm and I was stuck at his place. To pass the time, we drank and I ended up dancing. I never knew how turned on he was until I came back from the bathroom and there he was naked and nine inches of hard."

"I had never been with an experienced guy.

From that night on, I was strung out on him." Nicole smiled at that thought because she could relate. Shannon continued, "I hardly did my schoolwork. All I wanted to do was please him. The dancing got more provocative and his sex did too. Some stuff we did, I was really too drunk to remember. He asked me if would dance for his partners at the house one night for five hundred dollars a head. I made fifteen hundred dollars that night and Bernard was freakishly excited. The next time I danced the men brought their wives. It turned into an orgy. I didn't feel comfortable at first, but Bernard offered me a little pill with my drink. All I wanted to do was make him happy. He enjoyed other men having sex with me. He videoed their wives going down on me and we watched the video the next day as we had sex. This is what we did for almost two years; other couples, toys, orgies, whatever he wanted. He even paid for plastic surgery to get my breast the size he liked. He said bigger breast would make the other couples want me more. Life was good. I was still in school, enjoying karate and living like a sex goddess."

Shannon let out a sigh before she continued, "On one of our orgy nights, no wives showed up, just the husbands. I was nervous that night because I was going to do belly dancing and wanted the girls to join me. Bernard gave me some pills and some shots. The music came on and I gave in to the rhythm. Bernard was so turned on, he did me right there in front of everybody. Live action porno and he was so good that night. I climaxed countless times. With B's approval, one of the guys joined us during sex, to suck him off. When Bernard was done, he called for another guy to take his place. Then another. That night was like a sex dream. I only remember everything felt so good and Bernard was happy. I woke up the next afternoon sore with three thousand dollars in an envelope."

"When I graduated, I was ready to get serious about life. The party life was over and I needed a change. Our life was changing. Bernard didn't seem pleased with just me anymore. He always needed an audience. The group of usual guys or swingers, a mirror, video feedback, anything. I did anything he wanted to keep him happy but there was always a need for more. We would go out to dinner and come home to his partners and friends screwing all over the house. I would join in to keep the peace. The one time I said no, he slapped me, handcuffed me and let everybody in the group do what they pleased to me."

"His partners started bringing girlfriends and mistresses to the group. I could not tell the wives. Toys came with the girlfriends. Bernard loved these toys and wanted to use them with or without the group. I parted ways with the group when Bernard physically held me down so one of the new girls could try out a strap on. The next day, I packed my stuff and left. Bernard tried to get me to come back. I even went back a couple of times; only to leave over the same 'forced' issue. In the hospital one day, I saw one of the partners' wives. She told me they missed me. I told her everything about the girlfriends. She told me about the video recordings, I never knew about. I confronted him about it after class and he did not deny it. The partner's wife left him and moved in with me. Our friendship blossomed. Eventually, she moved to Cali and I stayed."

"Why do you stay at the school?" Is all Nicole could manage to say.

"Because he'll show the videos on the net or

somewhere if I leave. He likes having me at the karate school, in his sight, under his control. But if I ever get those recordings or any of the other hundreds my ex-girlfriend says he has, I'll make sure he will never make another video. I will have something on him for once. Then maybe I will blackmail him, take the money and move to Florida."

"Bastard."

"I will do anything to get him back for what he did to Amanda. She doesn't even know how many people there really were. I want to help you but your actions up to this point are useless, unless you are going to gain his trust by giving him that hard-core stuff he likes. Then, he will feel that he has you under his control." Shannon sounded almost matter of fact.

Nicole admired her logic, "Point taken. Solutions?"

"None yet. Give me a minute to come up with something he likes that's creative and I'll let you know after class this week."

"Make it soon because a minute is all we have." Nicole shot Shannon a worried look.

Shannon came up with a plan that Nicole thought would almost work. Her only discomfort was the amount of drugs needed to carry this off. Shannon was sure Nicole could get the drugs at Bernard's house. Nicole had a different idea. Otherwise, she agreed to Shannon's plan. The two women needed Billy as usual. With a two-week deadline, the plan was in motion.

Nicole had Billy tell Bernard he was going out of town for a few days. Then, she followed up with hyping up this time for the two of them. Next, she put a wrought iron bed in her guest room. Nicole spent a week delivering Bernard different items such as thongs and rose petals. She bought a cheap nonstick saucepan and anti nausea transdermal patches. Finally, she and Billy spent in Friday night the kitchen diluting mushrooms to the right consistency for their purposes of the night with Bernard.

Saturday night Nicole was jittery. She felt like she needed the Rohypnol. Wine at dinner eased her a little bit. Together, they polished off a whole bottle. He drank more than her, as usual. Bernard brought his overnight bag with the items she sent. Once in her guest room, Bernard was clearly impressed by the set up. He pulled her close and began kissing her passionately. It was hard for Nicole to restrain and reciprocate at the same time. She knew Billy had an eye on her.

"Are you ready?"

"Oh hell yeah."

"Be naked." Nicole picked up the bag and exited. She came back dressed in all white. White fishnets, garter belt and leather bra. New was the thing she had not sent him, a white wig.

"Oh shit!"

"You like?"

His answer was to kiss her again. This time by rubbing his palms against the leathery material, "Damn you are sexy."

"It's part of the show."

"Show?"

"Yeah baby. Lay back and watch." She

guided him to bed. He seemed too steady for her so she gave him a big sip of wine. She laid him back with a kiss, "You trust me baby?"

"Yeah, why?"

"Trust this will be the best ass you have ever had." Then she kissed Bernard hard, biting his bottom lips. She shifted up and buried his face in her breasts. While he kissed her cleavage, she held his head in place and slipped the fingertip size patch behind his ear. Next she took his right hand and clamped his wrist to the hidden hand cuffs on the bed.

"What?" was Bernard's slightly delayed response.

"Bernard, it is part of the show. I won't hurt you. Much." She slapped his thigh with a little force.

"As long as I get to hurt back."

"You do have one free hand. Finish your wine while I get the lights. Drink it and you get pre show activities."

The rest of his wine was gone in a gulp. With courage fueled by a mix of lust and power rush, Nicole began to dance as she and Shannon had practiced. She gyrated against his erection until his toes curled. During her kisses on his thighs, his hand came up to try to force her mouth on his rock hard member She bit the tender spot on the inside of his thigh causing him to jerk. "No hands on the wig."

"Oh sorry, baby. You are good. I want it just like the other-"

In a flash Nicole rose to kiss him to cut him off, knowing Billy was within earshot. Against his mouth she murmured, "Don't mention that again or I won't do again."

His only response was to nod. Knowing he was ready, Nicole got up with a smile. She turned off the night lamp and left the bed. Next she turned on the speakers and hit the light switch. Instantly, a luminescence black light bathed the room, not only making Nicole's garments glow, but also revealing iridescent lips and fake eyelashes and henna like design on her abdomen around her belly button.

She began to dance the more seductive dance Shannon taught her. Stiff at first but she loosened up as the music flowed. She climbed on the bed and pushed him into sitting position for a lap dance. His free hand went wild, scratching, slapping and groping. A few times she grinded backwards in his lap as his erection rubbed against her butt cheeks. When she saw Billy outside the door watching, she winked and licked her lips. She knew he was masturbating. Nicole turned around and kissed Bernard.

"You like? Want more?"

"Um huh." His eyes were all glassy.

Nicole hopped off the bed and out the room. Nicole's body double came back in with identical costume, down to same henna like design Nicole had around her navel. Without a word, she got on the bed and took him in her mouth. From the door, Billy and Nicole watched Shannon work on Bernard. It was like a live porn flick-exotic, hot, sensual and sultry. Nicole felt Billy press himself against her ass. His fingers teased her already stimulated breast. Looking at Shannon riding Bernard backwards, he whispered in her ear, "I think we can do better than them."

With dancer precision movements, Billy pivoted Nicole and lifted her onto him. She wrapped her legs around his waist as he glided her up and down in a beautifully satisfying rhythm. Nicole communicated that she wanted to finish on top so they slid to the floor to accommodate her desire. They moved together as one in synchronized movements; eyes locked together and whispers of love while totally oblivious to Shannon's mission.

In the other room, Shannon could not get distracted by the couple in the hallway. Bernard needed to climax before he passed out or Nicole would have bigger problems. She went to work on his old likes, allowing him to smack her ass hard enough to bruise. She sat on his face as he bit and sucked her into mindless orgasms. His fingers surged in and out of her ass. After her third orgasm, Shannon moved her wet hot muscles from his face to this erection and rode him like old times. She repressed the memories with each smack on the ass. With his free hand, he urged her hips faster. His vulgar pleas for release were delivered weakly, almost as if he was crying. His begging for release was mixed with babbling about his dead wife being in the corner. Through hallucinations and tears, he finally came. Moments later, Shannon heard the couple verbally signaling they were done.

Shannon lifted Bernard's hand only to see it drop like a stone. Out cold as expected. More emotionally exhausted that anything, she made a beeline for Nicole's extra bathroom to compose herself. It was after two in the morning when the three sat down in Nicole's kitchen, relieved the deed was done.

Shannon was the first to break the silence, "That was creepy toward the end. Did you hear him call me Rita? I am glad that is over, so now what?"

"Now the rest is up to me," Nicole replied heavily.

"Well, what's wrong?"

"Everybody has done their part and I just hope I can do mine."

Billy held her hand. "Look babe. So far you have done everything to a tee. You have to keep going. If Bernard ever found out what's been going on, he will ruin you, might even kill you and everyone involved. You can do this."

Nicole resigned with a nod.

"What about the morning?" Shannon asked.

"I'll do him the same way he did Amanda, leave him with a note and a used up feeling.

The last episode with Nicole (Shannon) left Bernard feeling satisfied but taunted. As much as he liked Nicole's kinkiness, he did not get it on video, nor was he in control. He never felt in control with her. It was new and scary, but somehow felt strangely comfortable to him. Also, Bernard had feelings for Nicole that went beyond the need to possess her. He had felt this way only twice before: with his first wife, Sherry, and his last wife, Rita.

Tuesday's class was great. Bernard was in an exceptional mood. He even supervised the after class sparring workout. Wednesday, Nicole was meeting Pamell downtown Scarborough and saw Pfegan going into the town's favorite wing place. When her meeting was over, she went in hoping to ask the other woman about the upcoming competition in Virginia. Pfegan was tucked away in a booth under the stairs. Nicole was surprised to see her drinking what looked like a daiquiri in the late afternoon. Pfegan was shocked to see Nicole as well.

"Girl, what are you doing here?"

"Just relaxing this afternoon," Pfegan seemed nervous. She realized what this must looked like. Blushing, she glanced at her drink and said, "It's a virgin."

Nicole shrugged, "Going to Virginia this weekend?"

"I don't know. I thought I might go as a judge."

"Your hubby judging too?"

The younger women sighed, "He's working again."

"I hate that. He's a great competitor. His *kata* with the bo staff is trophy material. Did Bernard teach him that one?"

"No, your boyfriend did not. As a matter of fact, he was against Scott learning anything other than what he wanted him to know," the younger woman spat out.

"Wait. I just asked about a *kata* and your

husband. Where does the hostility come in against me or my *sensei*, not boyfriend, Bernard?"

Tears streamed down Pfegan's face. "I'm sorry. Scott just works so hard and we still aren't successful."

"What are you talking about?"

Pfegan's expression changed from sadness to awe. "You really didn't know Scott works for Bernard some weekends? That's how we pay for the infertility treatments that insurance does not cover."

"That's nice but what does Bernard get out of this?" Nicole asked leery.

"I don't really know. Scott never tells me. Sometimes, he flies Bernard in person to different cities and sometimes, he just picks up boxes. Antiques I think. Scott really doesn't like to talk about it. He knows Bernard makes me feel uncomfortable ever since Rita passed. That's why I don't come to class without him."

"Why do you stay? There are other karate schools."

"You wouldn't believe the things Bernard says to the other schools about his students. Other schools don't even want us to join. I don't know if you are friendly with Alexis Shaw, but she attempted to leave once. She tried to switch to judo. The instructor told her flat out he needed to keep things on a positive note with Bernard and could not accept her in his school."

"I didn't know," Nicole was amazed.

"I'm beginning to wonder how true the rumors are. You and Bernard are not close at all are you?"

Nicole had to make a quick decision: confess or lie. "If I tell you its complicated what would you think?"

Pfegan chuckled, "That you answered my question with a question."

"It's not what you think."

Pfegan laughed then, "Oh I know it's not! You're not in college and you're not stupid. His position and money have no lure for you. What is it?"

"You know about the college girls too?"

"Know about, hell, I was almost one. Nicole where have you been? I've been at the school fifteen years on and off. I was a university student from the area. I grew up in Tetterton, so I commuted. My sorority sister and I started out under Craig. We graduated as yellow belts and left the college recreation center gym to go to Bernard's school. I was impressed by Bernard's free flowing generosity to the students. He always wanted to go out after class. I wanted to go too but had to go home. My sorority sister would talk about what a great time I missed, what a wonderful man he was. I went out with them a couple of times. Bernard was dancing and kissing all the girls."

"Scott transferred to our school as a green belt from the Silver City affiliated school after I had been in class a year. He found out about the school after he saved Bernard from a boating mishap. He was so quiet and skillful. He rose through our ranks so quick that in less than ten months, he was testing for brown. I found myself gravitating to him after class. I asked him to be my self-defense partner for my green belt. We began dating after my test."

"My sorority sister stopped coming to class

rather suddenly. She moved out of the sorority house into a private suite on campus. We didn't see too much of each other for a while because I was getting serious with Scott. I did see her during pledge week. I asked what happened, why she had stopped coming to class. She told me that Bernard began flirting with her after class. He also questioned her constantly about me. Dana also said when they had sex he would call her my name by mistake. The night she spoke up and insisted he stop calling her my name turned into her a mistake. He got super rough and she called it quits."

"I thought nothing more about it. I graduated and worked two jobs. I had little time for karate. Scott and I got married on a cruise. When we got back, he began to train for his black belt and I began looking for commercial artist jobs. We tried to start a family once my job was secure. After a year Scott promoted to black belt, no baby. I fell into depression and gained forty pounds. Scott was trying to get me back in class. When my doctor said losing weight would help our process, I went back to class. Review at first, then I trained for my black belt. I was promoted and lost sixty pounds. Still no baby. Then we started going through test and treatments. Did I mention the bills that go along with that? Scott had to work a second job to cover our expenses. No more karate."

"Bernard was running short handed at the *dojo*. Craig was busy in the department, Alexis was out on maternity leave. He needed teachers. He asked Scott to stay if he got him another type of job. The rest is history."

"Just like that? Why don't you like being in class around Bernard alone?"

"Well a few months back, Bernard came to me and suggested that Scott's little swimmers were the problem. He offered to use his own sperm, our little secret, to give us a child. I never said a word to Scott. He would kill Bernard. Then there would be no husband, no baby, and no future. I stay to keep the peace until we get pregnant. Then we can leave the school and Scott is done with Bernard."

"Pfegan, I never knew." Nicole wanted to hug the other woman, but instead reassured her things would work themselves out.

Nicole's heart was heavy in relaying Scott

and Pfegan's story to Billy during their bubble bath. Her voice wavered with ambiguity when she told him about Bernard helping out with the medical bills.

Billy asked, "Baby, what do you want to do about it? Talk to Bernard about the things Pfegan confided in you?"

"Of course not. I just want to help them, even if it is only to offer therapy services or something. They are our friends, Billy. They are like family."

"I know." Billy warned, "Be careful; business and friends don't mix. I know you have a big heart that wants to help, but right now is not the time. We have to stay on course."

"I know. We are so close. So let's stay the course. Now it is time for our big announcement."

Hati

Tuesday night, Bernard told Nicole that he would be gone to New York until Sunday. She responded by lying to him saying she was leaving for Texas after class. He was generally disappointed but perked up when she talked about meeting with him on Sunday night.

Thursday night she wore a diamond ring to class and fended off questions by saying it was just a ring.

Sunday night, Nicole was nervous. Bernard called around 5:00 pm and showed up with take out at 8:00 pm with Thai takeout. They drank almost half the bottle of wine before Nicole began to cry. Immediately, Bernard inquired why.

"Billy asked me to marry him. He gave me a ring and everything."

Bernard was in awe, "When. . . What. . . Why would he do that?"

"I don't know!" Nicole wailed, "I told him about us weeks ago. I have not taken any of his calls. Last week, he showed up after class with a ring and begged me to marry him. He said you were not the kind of guy for me and if I continued to see you, I would end up hurt."

Bernard's shock turned to uneasy anger, "What did you say?"

"No! Of, course."

"Well, why are you upset?"

"Because I thought you would be mad. I didn't want you to think I encouraged him in any way." Nicole cried harder, making a true spectacle.

Bernard's anger dissolved at her tears. He slid over and hugged her gently. "Oh silly woman. I would never think that. However, I will speak with Billy before the next class. I can also bar him from the school and get a restraining order for you."

"That's too much," Nicole smiled weakly.

He kissed her forehead, then the tears in her eyes and finally captured her mouth.

Immediately desire sprang in him, driven by wine and her frailty. He moved to get her in a better position. She surprised him by sliding to the floor on her knees and unzipping his pants. This sleek and submissive move brought a pleasing grin to Bernard's face. Finally, he thought, she's completely mine, mind and body. He lay back on the sofa and enjoyed the rhythm of her soft mouth. Her skills improved over the time they had been together. He did not even mind the gentle nibbling on his head.

"Please come in my mouth," she begged.

Bernard could not believe his ears. If another man proposing made her behave this way, he would have TJ ask her to marry him tomorrow. "You bet baby. You just keep on sucking. Make your master happy."

Her pace increased into frenzy. She didn't mind Bernard grabbing her hair. It was so good; he could hear his heart pounding in his ears. Time seemed to slow down, then speed up. This whole thing felt like the best trip ever. When Bernard felt his muscles tighten so hard the skin ached, he knew he could not contain it anymore.

"Oh God baby. I love you. Here I come!"

With his hot semen, he felt blood rushing in his head making his ears pound. Nicole was licking and nibbling him while squeezing his balls, intensifying his organism. Bernard felt so drained; he looked down enough to blow her a kiss, then laid back limply on the sofa and dozed off. He was so out of it, he did not even feel Nicole stick a syringe at the base of his deflated erection.

He was woken up by a gentle nudging. Groggily he looked up at a fully dressed Nicole. Her appearance eased away some of fog in this mind.

"Where are you going?"

"To the hospital. One of my patients has had an episode. I'm going to assess the situation and decide whether hospitalization for the rest of week is the next step," she let out a long tired sigh.

"How long will you be there?"

"All night maybe." She held up her briefcase, "So I came prepared."

Slowly, Bernard got up and stretched. He was a little unsteady on his feet. "You must have sucked my brains out."

"Funny."

At the door Bernard turned and said, "Seriously, I meant what I said. I do love you and I will take care of this situation with Billy. Perhaps even today." He kissed Nicole and left.

Nicole got in her car and left, going in the other direction.

The next day Nicole got a call at her office from Barbara that there had been an accident early in the morning and Bernard was dead. All Nicole could do was cry. She cried because Bernard would not be in her life anymore, because Billy was free, because Amanda was vindicated, but mainly because the storm was over.

She rescheduled her afternoon appointments. The majority of her sobs had subsided and she was composed when a friend, in the form of a detective, showed up at her office. Craig Black had lines of worry creased in his brow. They embraced and Nicole felt Craig's shoulders sag.

"Hard job, uh?"

"You don't know the half. Today, I saw my mentor lying on a slab in the morgue. Then I have to come and question a good friend to piece together the puzzle that got him there."

"What do you mean? What do you need?" Nicole was genuinely puzzled.

"Was Bernard with you last night?"

"Yes and it was a bad night. I don't know if you knew, but Billy asked me to marry him. I told Bernard last night and we broke up. He was drinking; it ended badly," Nicole replied, hoping she sounded convincingly sad.

"Did you have sex?"

"Yes. Why?"

"DNA test will bring questions. That's all."

"Billy won't know will he?"

"Not unless you tell him because quite frankly, that is not my business to tell. Nicole, I

know Bernard had a dark side and did some . . .
things. Things I hope you did not do with him.
But I have to ask, did you do drugs with him
last night?"

"Drugs?"

"A vile of coke was found in the car."

"No. I have never done drugs. Nor have I
seen him do drugs. Is that how he died, an
overdose?"

"No. Massive internal injuries. The car
jumped the highway and dropped down an
embankment. He was thrown from the car. On
site estimated cause of death, a broken neck
probably with punctured lungs and massive
internal bleeding. Looks like he did not die on
impact, he tried to crawl to the car, probably for
his phone to call for help. Didn't make a foot.
Autopsy will give a more specific cause of
death." Craig looked a little pale reciting the
details.

"When I said I never saw Bernard do drugs,
that was not entirely true. I have seen him take
ecstasy and mushrooms. God knows what else.
He does things that I don't approve of or want

to hear about." Nicole looked down.

"Nicole, how could you turn a blind eye to his behavior?"

"What was I suppose to do Craig? Come to school and announce that our beloved *sensei* does illegal drugs? And I know this because he takes them so we can screw like bunnies."

Craig resigned, "No, I guess you couldn't. But Nicole if you knew about B, why did you date him? I have been at that school longer than you and most of the other black belts and the things I have seen and heard lead me to believe Bernard treated his women like old toys. How could you even think of switching gears from Billy to Bernard?"

Nicole gave Craig a whimsical smile, "Everybody gets caught up. Billy wasn't treating me right; he blamed Bernard for the misery in his life. As a way to get back at him, I went out with Bernard. Surprisingly, I liked him. He was fun. He was different, adventurous. But the drugs and wild sexual requests did me in because I could not do the drugs with him. I grew up seeing drugs ruin my parent's marriage so it was never my scene.

Much as I cared for him, I could not lose my whole career behind attempting to enhance our sex life. I would not video record, dress up or swing with other couples. So when Billy and I talked again, I was ready to leave. Telling Bernard was hard. If I hadn't told him last night, he might be alive now," she finished quietly.

"Come on Nicole, don't blame yourself. You didn't make him use drugs. And don't give another thought to it. Bernard may have been one way to you and the women in class, but he was another way for the guys. The Lord works in mysterious ways." Craig rose to leave, "Well, like I said, don't blame yourself. If the department has any more questions, I'll contact you again. Barbara will be in touch with all of us soon I'm sure."

It felt funny that the place where they sparred, sweated and learned to hone artistic movements to killer precision was now that place where they memorialized their founder. Class had been cancelled until further notice.

The mood was a strange mixture of sadness, respect and tension. The crowd consisted of students, friends, family, and business associates. Everyone from circuit court judges to kick boxers came to show their respect to a great figure in Scarborough.

After almost everyone had departed, only the martial artist students remained. Barbara pulled Nicole over to the side for a moment. "We need to talk. Can you do the little Italian place up the street from here tomorrow for lunch?"

"Yeah, what's up?"

"His will."

"1:00 pm okay?"

Barbara nodded.

Nearby them, Drew was asking Rocky about the future of the karate school.

"I don't know."

"Rocky, this is the time to seriously think about the expansion and promotion plans," Drew insisted.

"Drew," Clay interrupted, "this is not the time for this discussion."

"Yeah, well when is? Ever since I became a black belt, I begged for this school to grow. I asked to spearhead the project, but was denied. I'm not trying to change *sensei's* system, but in order for this school to be formidable, it has to embrace different ideals and procedures."

"My uncle built this school and founded this style. Who the hell are any of you to change decades of his hard work?" Clay fumed.

"Your uncle and Rocky. And if your uncle, my godfather, had given any weight to Rocky's voice in how things were run, our class size would double and our reputation would be reestablished," Drew shot back.

The remaining students began to gather around the two arguing men.

"Bernard ran this school just fine for years." Clay's voice was rising.

"Bernard used this school. *Shihans* as far as South Carolina knew that."

"I will not let you slander his name; not yet

an hour after his service." Clay moved toward Drew, who was already taking off his jacket.

"Enough!" Vanessa stepped between them, her icy tone making both men literally freeze. "This is not the time or place and arguing between the two of you is not going to resolve any past or future issues of this school. I have been in this system less than a year and have seen the same things that you who have been here a dozen years have seen and chosen to turn a blind eye. I have also learned to love the people that make this school more of a home away from home for anyone that crosses that threshold. Although we lost the patriarch of this family, we must learn to adapt as families do. This school, if we are to continue to be the family that Bernard sponsored, must keep his memory alive but not necessarily his ways. Think of this situation akin to the death of an abusive parent. After he's gone, do the kids continue in his ways by abusing themselves?"

With nods from the crowd, she continued, "This is a good place with great people, who I know from working with them, are trustworthy leaders. Lest, Bernard would not have promoted them to first rank and beyond. Now is the time to trust his judgment and faith in those people. Let the black belts decide the fate of this school."

Craig was the first to break the silence. "I have to think things over. I like what you said. Every word was true. Now I need time to go over my feelings for this school and the directions I would like for it to go."

"I think everyone needs to do that," Rocky added quietly, "Until further notice class will continue to be cancelled. I will be in touch with everyone."

Vanessa's comments started out lunch for Barbara and Nicole the next day. They had no sooner gotten their drinks when Nicole made the comment, "You know what Vanessa said was true."

"I know," Barbara concentrated on her menu.

"So what do you think?" Nicole pressed.

"I think that more than just Rocky needs to be making the decisions for the school. He was very much influenced by Bernard."

"I think Rocky is just defeated by years of dealing with Bernard. It's hard to fight against the current. You and I know from first hand experience how, um, difficult dealing with Bernard could be," Nicole sighed.

"I did like her idea of the black belts making the decisions. A board of trustees, per se. Last night, I counted nine black belts with five or more years. That's a good number." She took a sip of water. "Let's get down to business. Bernard was worth several million dollars. I found his will in the safe in his bedroom, but first I looked in his home office. I discovered a storage room with more than a thousand recordings of him having sex with women. He had them alphabetized, numbered and rated. Nicole, I saw names of people I know. Some of his former clients, girls from the office and class, a former assistant district attorney and those are just the names I know. Some were just labeled university girl 120 and had an episode code like S&M, BON, or GRP."

She paused long enough to order the Chicken Marsala and Nicole ordered steak. "I have my reasons for hating Bernard to a certain degree, but if the police get those videos, his name will be ruined. I talked to Craig and as soon as the autopsy results are in, there will be more questions."

"Why?" Nicole interrupted.

"Craig said that Bernard had additional chemicals in his system other the cocaine and ecstasy. His blood alcohol content was pushing the legal limit. Anyway, I need your help. I need to destroy the videos but write down the names of the people so I can set up a fund to at least compensate these women for their pain."

"I know that wasn't in his will."

"No it was not. But after Clay, Drew and Sherry all got his various estates and Rocky got the school, I was to inherit the remaining bulk of his fortune and the law office."

Surprised, Nicole said, "He left you all that?"

"Me and my boys. You forget I was his conscience for over twenty years. Not only did I help him build his business but also ran his business. It was time for my hard work to pay off. Plus, I've decided to go back to law school with my new fortune. Hell, I feel like I know enough over the years to be a lawyer, might as well make it official."

"Well congratulations. When do you want to do this?"

"Friday night. The reading of the will is set up for Monday."

"Friday night at 6:00 pm. I have a feeling this will take all night." The rest of the meal was spent talking about the ideas for the school.

Ku

Friday night came in a flash. Nicole drove up to the house she had been to only a handful of times. Barbara led her to a huge study that looked like something out of a movie. Nicole was shocked when Barbara pulled open a section of what appeared to be books to reveal a space the size of a half bath.

"Nicole, I think you better have a closer look." Nicole peered in the space to see that it had been looted. What was once countless videos now had large holes in some spaces. Videos were skewed all over the floor. "The video equipment is gone as well."

Across from the wall of videos were shelves of toys. Strap-ons, leather mask, spiked collars, clamps, scarves, paddles, creams, bondage straps, a vinyl body suit, paints, rings, and things Nicole was not sure were made in this country.

"Is any of that stuff missing?"

"I don't know. I don't even know what half of that stuff is."

Nicole laughed, "Half the stock of every kinky adult store from here to Vegas."

Both women got a laugh out of that, then set about on their most unpleasant task. During breaks, Nicole wandered the house. It was truly glamorous. Nicole had never been in his bedroom. The furniture was large and dark. His bed was the size of her truck. The room itself was as large as two libraries. His closet contained every suit imaginable. Nicole noticed he still had pictures of Rita up with a few of his parents and one of him and Drew's mother together. Bernard, even in death, still puzzled Nicole. How could someone capable of using the things in that little room, destroying the lives of Amanda, Pamell and countless others, have such love and compassion as to keep pictures of his dead wife still up?

Upon returning, Barbara was at Bernard's desk with a hammer. Nicole had to ask, "What are you doing?"

"I found a locked box inside his desk drawer."

"Well, you need a crow bar. Does he have one?"

It took Barbara so long to return, that Nicole started back on the remaining videos and writing down names. She came to a name she recognized: Shannon's. She counted over fifty tapes with Shannon's name. Shannon's first time; Shannon's birthday party; Bernard's birthday; Shannon, Bernard and Senator Chaz Alton; Shannon's first swing party; Shannon, Bernard, Ron, Randy, Grayson and Luke; Shannon's S & M night; the list went on and on. Nicole not only recognized Senator Alton's name, but a past university chancellor, current district attorney, three judges and quiet a few prominent females as well. Poor Shannon. After all of this, she still agreed to help Nicole.

Loud cracking and a pop broke Nicole's trance. She went out to see Barbara, crow bar in hand, looking into the desk box which was filled with audio tapes, two stacks of bills and two keys. Some of the audio tapes had names of people from the karate school: Scott, TJ, Billy, then Vice Chandler Mackey, Dick Cox, Coach Von Lockhart, and Curtis Mette. Barbara picked up the tape with her ex-husband's name on it with shaky hands.

"Barbara, I think you should take that and the keys home. Listen to it when you're a little calmer."

Barbara looked suddenly tense, "I think you're right."

The two women worked until midnight. They counted over five hundred videos; much of which was shredded there in the library's shredder. Barbara had several bags of shredded material in her truck and Nicole several in hers. When the shredder died, the women had to take a few boxes of tapes and CDs home to finish shredding individually. Nicole took the audiotapes and cash while Barbara took her one tape and the keys to whatever safety deposit box. The night ended on a quiet note with a hug and a promise to contact the other when the work was done.

The first official black belt council meeting was a traditional one. Everyone was dressed in traditional white *gi* and black belts. They sat on the floor, cross-legged and in order. As the eldest black belt and co-founder of the school, Rocky called the meeting to order. Before opening the floor he announced Alexis would not be joining them due to a family emergency out of town. Next he solicited open comments from the black belts in accordance to rank.

Craig: "This is a strong, thorough and respected style. To regain the respect we once had as a reputable martial arts school, the promotion policy must be changed."

Barbara: "The family atmosphere needs to remain. That is one of our strengths. Understand that families have problems as will we. Families work through difficult times, as will we."

TJ: "Enrollment needs to increase for the school to stay lucrative. The community reputation is damaged. The relationship with the university is in bad shape. Dan's class is struggling. Relations in the local, state and martial arts community need to improve. Reputation improves, enrollment improves."

Scott: "Changes take work. Every one of us as black belts has to decide if we are going to be dedicated to the changes that need to take place. Even when and especially when change is uncomfortable."

Pfegan: "Memorialize does not mean idolize. Plus, everyone who was personally trained by Bernard respected his dedication and hard work to his discipline. Yet, this school must now grow. We cannot clearly see the path to future success if we are constantly looking back to old unsuccessful ways."

Drew: "The school needs a major overhaul. Promotion policy, image and attitudes. We all have expertise in certain areas creating a unique and diverse skill set to pull instruction from. That is a strong point that will set this school apart from other schools."

Clay: "My uncle's memory should be respected within the changes. As the founder of this system, we should always honor him. We should stick to the older, more traditional ways."

Nicole: "The school is a family to all of us. I remember times when this school was a refuge to those who needed a focus and a purpose. The great things Bernard did to foster this family away from family should be remembered by honoring him. However, the discriminatory processes such as promotions and partnerships should be changed. A wise teacher once prophesized that if one continues to do what they are doing, they will continue to get what they are getting. Let us move forward being wise, not foolish."

Rocky: "I listened to all of your comments. I founded this school as well as Bernard. My blood, sweat and tears went into this school. It hurt me to watch the downward spiral of this school and its reputation. I have seen great students disheartened and poor students breeze through to get undeserved belts. The promotion policy will change in order for this school to continue. For this school to continue, the black belts must commit the time to the changes we agree upon. I work out of town as many of you know and I know you all have full time jobs. That being said, all of you will be called upon at times to help out. I know all of your specialties, backgrounds and abilities. The various approaches and styles will keep classes interesting. Finally, before we start on this rebuilding process keep this in mind: we think of this building as a home and each other as family. As we work out our future, keep an open heart to change as your roles will change to accommodate the common goal of a successful school."

The next two hours were spent hashing out complaints, suggestions and problems. There were tense moments and quiet lulls. In the end, a rough outline was finished. The council agreed to meet once a month until the school ran smoothly again. When they were dismissed, Nicole hurried so she could catch Scott and Pfegan. They were in the parking lot.

"Scott! Hey Scott wait up," she called.

Scott stopped. "What is it Nicole? We're tired and Pfegan is hungry."

"I just wanted to give you something." She handed him the audiotape wrapped in silver tape.

"What is this?"

"I don't know what's on yours, but Bernard had a similar one made of a conversation with Billy. If it is along those same lines, then consider your debt to him paid in full."

Scott looked at her wearily.

"I didn't listen to it and that is the only copy that I know of."

Finally, Scott said, "You know I was waiting for this moment. When he died I held my breath waiting for something like this to surface and destroy me. Some way I felt like he still controlled me even in death. I just don't know what to say."

Nicole laughed, "There's nothing to say. Go home and work on your family."

Scott broke into a wide grin. He opened Pfegan's door. "Babe, can we tell Nicole our good news?"

Pfegan blushed. "I am pregnant! Almost ten weeks. We weren't going to tell anybody until I was out of danger."

Nicole smiled back at them. "Congratulations! I won't say a word."

"Thanks."

As Scott got in the car, he paused and said, "Thank you Nicole. Really. I can go into parenthood without any shameful strings attached. Thank you so much."

Nicole winked and went toward her own car. Nicole's next person to see was Shannon. She called en route to the apartment Shannon now shared with Amanda. When she came to the door, Nicole stood with two boxes.

"Been to class?"

"No. The first official black belt council meeting." Nicole shoved the two boxes inside.

"Anything good?"

"Not yet. Amanda here?

"No. Why?"

"Because these boxes are for you and I don't know if you want her to see any of this . . . mess."

"What is it?"

Nicole sat on the closest chair. "They are the videos Barbara and I confiscated from Bernard's house. I don't know how many there were in all. When we got there, someone had looted a large number of videos according to Barbara. I got all the ones with your name on them and brought them to you to personally destroy. A little mental freedom tool."

Shannon's face went slack and a tear escaped. She breathlessly said, "I don't know what to say."

"There's nothing to say. As far as I'm concerned, I owe you big time. I could not have gone through this last leg without you. You really made all the pieces fall in place. Thank you for all you did."

"That wasn't for you. That was my own personal revenge. For once, it was that bastard lying there drugged senseless, helplessly being taken advantage of by me. In a sick and twisted way, that was my mental freedom. That was the first time he never knew what hit him. But I got to confess, he was good for old time sakes. I had mixed emotions, knowing what he did to Amanda but also knowing what we did had to be done. Did you ever actually do Bernard?"

Nicole nodded.

"He was packing, could go for hours and that tongue was nothing else in this world. Best lover I had, while it was good. He would give my girlfriends a run for their money. Does Billy know?"

"Nope. He would kill me. Even in this circumstance. He wouldn't understand that I had to do it for the good of the cause."

Shannon burst out laughing, "Yeah right! Nicole, I have to ask, did you kill him?"

Nicole pretended to be wounded, "Heavens no. It seems our Bernard was an undercover drug user. All those drugs in his system at one time were more than he could take. After I told him Billy and I were getting married, he got doped up, we had goodbye sex and he went home. On his way home, he lost control of his car and died."

Shannon laughed again, "That's your story? Your real story?"

"And I'm sticking to it."

Shannon hugged Nicole. She hugged back and said, "Be thinking about testing for black belt. Pick a good self defense partner like Drew or Scott."

As Nicole turned to the door, Shannon asked, "Why did you ask was Amanda here?"

Nicole sighed, "I asked because I didn't want to have to tell her that I couldn't find her video."

❧

"So this is where cops go to drink?"

"Nicole, what are you doing here?"

"Let's say, I just felt like eating at a greasy Greek hole in the wall close to the station."

Craig gave a sideways glance, "Right."

"I came here to drop something off." She slid the audiotape wrapped in sliver paper over to him.

"What's this?"

"A little something I found at Bernard's house," she shrugged.

"So it was you. The officers said someone had been in the house. What were you doing there? Other than interfering with an open investigation."

"Helping Barbara clean up Bernard's image."

Craig seemed shocked, "Damn Barb too? Lot of that going around these days."

Interested, Nicole said, "Yeah?"

"Yeah. Investing officer found a tape of Bernard torturing and sodomizing some girl in the DVD player. The captain wanted me to look at the DVD with him to see if it was someone he was dating. I thought it might be you. But it was that pretty little Black university dancer that came to the school for awhile, Coco something. I remember thinking she had potential. Actually seeing Bernard dehumanizing her made me physically sick."

"I talked with my captain and begged him not to let this go public. Families would suffer. The captain did not respond immediately. Instead, he just pulled Bernard's toxicology screen out of his jacket and tells me what's in it. There was found enough HGB in his system in addition to all those other illegal drugs to revival any small dealer in Scarborough."

Craig shifted in his seat uncomfortably, "My

captain continued by telling me some of the stories he heard about women, especially the college students, being raped around Scarborough for years. Once, it was thought Scarborough had a serial rapist. Captain heard the guy's name began with a B or V. Department cold case files has a small section of cases with DNA and women who can't testify because they had no memory or were just plain scared. My captain was tempted to see if Bernard's DNA would match any on file."

"Now my pleading with him doubled. Just let the dead stay dead, I tried to reason with the captain. Finally, he agreed to 'losing' the video and the HGB but keeps the 'shrooms, ecstasy and cocaine as evidence that helps the pathologist explain the drugs present in his system." After a pause to wet his throat with beer, Craig continued. "But something is not right here. If B was a drug user, he was the cleanest I know. No tracks anywhere except one between his toes and one on his junk."

"Maybe he needed a quick high. Shooting is quicker than lines," Nicole shrugged her shoulders.

"Or maybe you knew and didn't care to stop him," Craig eyed her carefully.

"Or maybe if you tell me what's on your tape, it will make the scales balance," Nicole replied in a low voice.

Craig plucked his tape. "Before I made detective, I did things for extra money because I was trying to finish my degree. This and that appeared and disappeared from the evidence locker. Bernard benefited but screwed me with this tape. You?"

"I knew Bernard did drugs. I might have helped him that night. I wanted him to have the best oral sex of his life." She left out the part where Billy assisted Bernard in his accident by forcing him off the road and down the embankment. The original lunge threw Bernard from the car all banged up. Billy finished completing the task by planting the coke, shooting a syringe full of the heroin between his toes. This added to the heroin and liquid E and heart medication she had already injected into his penis hours earlier. Billy recounted how Bernard suffered and how he called for help. Billy reported how with all those drugs in his system, Bernard became a gibbering idiot during his finally moments. He cursed, he cried, he tried to bargain with God. Billy left him wailing Rita's name. Neither Billy or Nicole breathed until Barbara called the next day.

"Did you know it would be his last? I mean his last high, sex with you, day on Earth?" Craig studied her.

"Nope. I only knew it would be my last time with him. I hate he had to go that way, but now the Pamell's and Amanda's of the world will be safe."

Craig looked shock, "Amanda? No, not Amanda. She was so . . . quiet."

"Hasn't been in class lately has she? She was utterly destroyed by him and his sick lust."

"No. How many more?"

"Hundreds maybe thousands."

"So did you kill Bernard? On purpose or by accident?" Craig leveled her with a straight look.

"Heavens no. That is my story and I am sticking to it," Nicole smiled.

"You didn't get any food."

"The subject of Bernard takes my appetite." She got up to leave, "See you in class next week."

"Thanks Nicole. Peace of mind is . . . well, priceless," he tapped his tape. "Just like you."

Ju

Tuesday night the class lined up in perfect row, according to the person on the left end. Rocky looked at the future of American Martial Arts Academy. Two rows of black belts, a row of brown belts, a row of green belts, orange and yellow belts, and two rows of white belts were present. All stood at attention beaming with pride. Rocky *reyed* the students in and class began.

Last night's class was great. It had been years since he performed yellow belt *katas*. TJ came to work at his basket store early today. The baskets in the front were just that, a front. In the back he sold sex toys, videos and had a communications board for those seeking swingers, multiple partners, role-playing and any other sexual fantasies that can come to a person's mind.

The store's appearance was more deceptive than just baskets made by and sold to help the local rehabilitation day treatment. It was actually an old drug store made into two stores by TJ sectioning off the front to a small front area and the back into spacious area that housed any and every adult possible fantasy. The downstairs which had once been for storage, now had a few rooms for select customers whose fantasies involved captivity and bondage. The upstairs housed his apartment which actually took up a decent sized section. There were other rooms for his other select customers who paid well for the space. In all, he had seven rooms that he charged 200 to 800 dollars a head, no questions asked except for IDs to check for age.

A reputable man that helped the disadvantaged in the community could not get caught with under aged people in his establishment. He could explain the second shop as a business, the meeting rooms as social networking, but fooling with the under aged was just bad for business. Even though his select customers like Bernard had privileged access to that particular aspect of his on demand services.

He walked past the wall of bondage and entered the code to open the door to his counter.

Whistling TJ stood in front of the bloodletting display and took out his keys. He lifted one of the hanging sword racks to reveal a hidden keyhole. The deadbolt slid back to open a room with several computer monitors and towers. Dozens of boxes from the home of the late Bernard Giovonni crowded the room.

Today, he launched his new website. He looked at the stacks of videos and DVDs he got from Bernard's library. Some of them were self-incriminating and those he would keep to just watch periodically or edit himself out before posting them on the internet. He knew the ones he shot that were good footage. He would sort through the others later.

He smiled at his dry, quirky humor as he downloaded a fifteen-minute clip of Bernard wearing the black mask doing some random girl with his strap-on trick. That was exactly what TJ named the clip-girl getting strap on trick. Thanks to Bernard, TJ would soon be comfortably wealthy with his brand new internet porn site business.

While the clip uploaded, he lit a blunt and viewed his favorite video to date on another screen, Amanda the zombie. He felt himself getting hard again just watching the three of them working her over. Slowly rubbing himself, TJ decided that Amanda was by far in his top three chicks he had ever done and if he could, he would definitely do her again. Even as a zombie he remembered how good it felt to do her, with ass cheeks spread and tight, wetness taking a beating from his pounding. His palm began to sweat from excitement as he slid his hand up and down his shaft, dark thoughts flooding in his mind. TJ wondered how hard it would be to find her and make her his own slave. As big as his place was nobody would ever find her. She could be chained in the basement or another room for months or years.

A slow sick smile spread across his face as the thought made him suddenly hard with anticipation. TJ stroked himself to a climax as the new planted seed took roots in his mind.

Epilogue

Nicole was helping Billy put up new shelves in their new shed when her cell phone rang. She hated leaving Billy to get it because they were finally make headway into this project. They were married two years before buying this house. She insisted they wait so it looked like they actually saved the deposit funds instead of what is really was, the money she found in Bernard's house that night.

With no questions asked or suspicions aroused, she was truly enjoying the house they had custom built. The karate family came to both their wedding and house warming. All of the black belts were still there. Some brown belts had since been promoted, namely Shannon and Billy. The school was in the black, reputable and expanded to offer new classes.

Nicole could not reach her actually phone so she answered by touching her earpiece. "Hello."

"Nicole, thank God you answered you phone," Barbara sounded breathless on the other end.

"Barbara, what's wrong?" Nicole was alarmed.

"You are not going to believe this but one of those damn missing videos is on the internet!"

"What!" Nicole exclaimed loud enough to bring Billy out of the shed. "How the hell-"

"I know! My youngest son and his college football teammates were messing around on internet porn sites and he recognized one of the college girls I used to give a ride to class. He was only ten and Bernard did not seem to mind him at the school. My son loved coming to class as much as he loved the fact I had to go on campus to what he thought was a skyscraper to pick up those the college students that needed a ride."

"He called tonight to tell me the red headed girl that I used to pick up from the 'skyscraper' was on a porn site about college girls. Dammit Nicole! I thought this whole thing was over. What the hell?"

Though her thoughts exactly, Nicole calmed Barbara down, promising they would handle this issue. When she got off the phone she relayed the whole conversation to Billy who echoed Barbara's sentiment.

Nicole hung her head, wanting to just sit in the grass and shut out the past. But she could not do that because someone out there was destroying lives. Twice. As if what Bernard did to those women was not enough. It was probably the same person that looted the video room.

"Honey, you don't have to do anything. You can talk to Barb. Convince her to let it go. Please let go," Billy knew his pleas were weak and in vain.

"You know I can't do that." Nicole walked away shaking her head, "Not while there's another predator just like Bernard. This time further traumatizing Bernard's victims and using his perversions to make money."

But who? Who had a house key **and** knew about the room?

Once inside the house, Nicole took a minute

to compose herself before dialing Shannon's number.

A heavy sigh escaped as Nicole wondered would they ever genuinely be free of Bernard or his legacy.

Nicole sighed again, this time with determination. There was work to be done.

THE END

(Or is it?)

ABOUT THE AUTHOR

Kumite is the author's third book. Though there are other materials and genres that Kerns has published, *Kumite* is the most graphic novel to date. A walk on the wild side from her usual contemporary women's romance thriller, card game how to and teenage fiction, *Kumite* takes Kerns' love for martial arts down a dark and twisted path. To add more of a personal touch, the sword in the cover belongs to the author. She is currently working on sequels to The Foreign Exchange and Kumite.

Check out her website at

www.seanscottkerns.com